# Thorn Ogres
# of Hagwood

## THE HAGWOOD TRILOGY
## BOOK ONE

## Robin Jarvis

Silver Whistle
Harcourt, Inc.
*San Diego   New York   London*

www.HarcourtBooks.com

Interior illustrations copyright © by Robin Jarvis, 1999

First published in Great Britain in 1999 by the Penguin Group,
Penguin Books Ltd, 80 Strand, London WC2R ORL, England
First U.S. edition 2002

*Silver Whistle* is a trademark of Harcourt, Inc., registered in the
United States of America and/or other jurisdictions.

Library of Congress Cataloging-in-Publication Data
Jarvis, Robin.
Thorn ogres of Hagwood/Robin Jarvis.
p.   cm.—(The Hagwood trilogy; 1)
"Silver Whistle."
Summary: The werlings, a peaceful group of forgotten forest creatures
whose only magic is the ability to change shapes, are unwittingly drawn
into the search for a valuable item stolen from an evil queen many years before.
[1. Fantasy.]   I. Title.   II. Series.
PZ7.J2965Th   2002
[Fic]—dc21      2001057606
ISBN 0-15-216752-8

Text set in Centaur MT
Designed by Cathy Riggs


A C E G H F D B


Printed in the United States of America

# Thorn Ogres
## of Hagwood

The Western Border of HAGWOOD

Lonely Mere

Barren Heath

Hazel

Doolan Elm

Tumpin Oak

Council Apple

Silent Grove

Hagburn

# Contents

# Characters

| | |
|---|---|
| GAMALIEL TUMPIN | *A young, clumsy werling beginning his first year of wergling school* |
| KERNELLA TUMPIN | *Gamaliel's bossy older sister* |
| FIGGLE AND TIDUBELLE TUMPIN | *Gamaliel and Kernella's parents* |
| YOORI MATTOCK | *A respected member of the presiding council of werlings* |
| MUFUS AND BUFUS DOOLAN | *Twin practical jokers; classmates of Gamaliel* |
| TERSER GIBBLE | *Great Grand Wergle Master and tutor of wergling* |
| FINNEN LUFKIN | *Young werling and classmate of Kernella Tumpin; supremely talented at the art of wergling* |
| TOLLYCHOOK UMBELNAPPER AND LIFFIDIA NEFYN | *Other classmates of Gamaliel* |
| RHIANNON | *High Lady; Queen of Hollow Hill* |
| THE SMITH | *The last of a race of dwarfs larger than werlings and smaller than humans* |

# Thorn Ogres
## of Hagwood

Beneath the early glimmering stars, the ancient, sprawling forest of Hagwood was crowded with menace and black branching shadow.

Within that smudging gloom, a solitary shape slipped swiftly. To the eaves of the wild forest it flitted, pausing only when it reached the edge of a steep bank and the chill air that arose from the invisible space below was filled with the slow music of water.

Here was the Hagburn, the stream that flowed close to the western border of that great tangled wood, and a pair of amber eyes glittered briefly as a proud head reared to gauge the distance.

In an instant it was done. Springing forward upon long, elegant legs, the creature leaped across the gulf and, with a flick of her splendid tail, alighted upon the far bank.

Quickly the hunter gazed about her. Within this narrow shoulder of the old realm, the trees grew tall and beautiful and did not strangle or jostle for room like those twisted giants she had left behind. A hushed calm lay upon this moonlight-dappled place, but there was no time to linger and savor these ravishing delights; her errand was too urgent.

For two days the vixen had remained close to the snug earth that she and her mate had clawed in the root-clogged ground of the forest. There she had patiently awaited his return, but that afternoon, as she tended to their two young cubs and listened to their hungry yelps, she had finally realized that she would never see the dog-fox again. It was she who now must provide, and her own empty stomach snarled within her. A substantial kill was needed that night, and she hastened her pace until the outermost oaks of Hagwood were in sight.

There, where the last shapely branches stretched out above an overgrown cinder track, she halted—ears erect. Alert and wary, the vixen appraised the immense emptiness before her.

Beyond the neglected road, a barren heathland reached into the darkness, but she knew that further still lay the Lonely Mere. With trembling nostrils she interrogated the drifting scents and caught the tantalizing fragrance of the remote, deep green water.

Contemplating the fat, fleshy duck that would soon be hers, the vixen was seized with a delicious thrill, and with an exhilarated bound, she shot from cover to gallop gladly across the track.

To the unwary the heath was a treacherous place where pits and shafts gaped in the broken ground, their slippery brinks concealed by weeds. Yet the vixen had often hunted here, gradually learning its secrets. Briskly she ran, expertly avoiding the hidden traps, the thought of the feast that awaited drawing her ever closer to the Lonely Mere.

An unearthly silence smothered the bleak desolation of that place, and when the ground became soft and damp beneath her paws, the vixen slowed her pace and halted. Then, stealthily, she began to creep forward.

The smell of the still, dank water was strong now; already the rough grasses and outlying clumps of thorn and briar were giving way to the gently swaying blades of the reeds.

Soon she would find her victim, some unsuspecting waterfowl dozing stupidly by the shallows. How swiftly she would pounce, her jaws snapping about a feathery neck as she delivered a violent, quacking death. The struggle would be fleeting, and with her teeth clamped around a juicy body, the duck's silly head wagging lifeless at her flank, she would trot back to the earth and share the succulent mouthfuls with her cubs.

The slightest of sounds caused her ears to flick in agitation, but she was too absorbed in her assassin's labor to pay it any heed.

Beneath her paws the soil had turned to mud, and black water seeped up into the prints she left behind. The edge of the dank mere was so close now, her quest would soon be over. No warning must be given; she must be silent like a shadow....

Again her ears jerked to attention, but this time she hesitated. The faint noise unsettled her, and she quickly glanced over her sleek shoulders.

Something was out here, close by—rustling through the grass behind her.

Her eyes shining and vigilant, the vixen scanned the night while her nostrils sought for any telltale scent.

Nothing.

If any creature was prowling the heath, then it was one she had never encountered before. Switching her head from side to side, she strained her ears to catch any further sound, but all she heard was the creaking of thorny branches, and a vague unease began to churn in her empty stomach. Instinct and experience warned that she was not the only predator abroad that night, and she sensed that from the concealing darkness, hostile eyes were watching.

Dread rapidly took the place of hunger. A sudden, awful fear seized her—all at once she felt alone and vulnerable, and the desire to flee that place utterly overwhelmed her.

Summoning her strength, the vixen steadied herself upon her long legs and tensed, preparing to leap forward and race back over the barren wilderness. Only then did she realize.

The dark landscape of the heath changed. Tangled shapes, blacker than the encompassing night, had moved. The thornbushes and knots of briar that she had so stealthily passed only minutes ago had shifted position. Whereas before they had been isolated shrubs scattered across the wasteland, they were now grouped together to form a dense thicket barring her retreat.

Taking a hesitant step closer, the vixen peered at that unnatural fence, confused and afraid. How had it happened? Who could have done this? Where in that expansive gloom was the mover of trees lurking?

Bewildered, she stared at those impenetrable barbed branches, anxious to find a way through, but there was none. In that spiky wall there was not a single gap, and she cast her desperate gaze back to the mere. She would have to wade through the water, perhaps even swim, to reach another stretch of the shore.

At once, there came the crackle of twigs, and the vixen whirled around to face the thorns again. Tentatively she began to back away, out to the water's edge—but then she saw it.

There was her chance. Within that prickly barrier was a narrow breach, just large enough for her to dart through. Panic had caused her to overlook it before, and now her heart leaped to find it.

Wasting no more time, she flung herself forward. Then it happened. Before she could tear through that inviting gap, two pale points of light snapped open in the dim dark ahead, and a thin, rasping voice began to hiss with cruel laughter.

At once, the heavy shadows all around glittered with countless pairs of luminous eyes, and the vixen's courage finally left her.

A terrified yowl issued from her throat as she lunged hopelessly for the gap; one more bound and she would be free. But just as she lowered her head to bolt beneath the thorns, there came a clattering of branches and the break in the hedge was no longer there. Briar and twigs now blocked the way, and unable to stop herself in time, the vixen went skidding and sliding right into the thicket's prickly heart.

Across the empty heath and the flat surface of the mere, her pain-filled yelps went sailing as a score of bitter spikes needled into her flesh. Vainly she wriggled to escape from the thorny darts that hooked into her skin, but the more she struggled, the closer and fiercer the capturing barbs gripped her.

Then the laughter began again.

It was louder now and composed of many hideous voices that crowed and cackled from every direction.

She wrenched her head aside to look on her captors, and the squeezing thorns ripped her cheek as she squirmed. At last the vixen beheld them, and her beautiful eyes grew dim with fear.

All around her the dense hedge was moving, rearing from the stubbly grass upon many stumpy legs. They were the thorn ogres, and the twisted boughs that crested their grotesque heads rattled together as they closed ever tighter about the stricken fox.

Pinned upon the deadly branches of the one that had captured her, she saw the other nightmares advance, and knew that her fight was over. From the swathing darkness misshapen limbs raked out, but she closed her eyes before the first brutal blow fell.

High into the chill night air her dying scream soared, and even in the depths of Hagwood, the ghastly shriek echoed through the ancient trees.

By the shore of the Lonely Mere the vixen perished, and as the frenzied claws ripped and tore at her wilting body, her very last thought was for her cubs—who would feed them now?

# CHAPTER I
# Gamaliel Tumpin

A golden dawn edged up over the rim of Hagwood. The new leaves of March made the forest roof glow a glorious green, and the morning resounded with joyous birdsong.

In the western corner of that vast woodland, other inhabitants were stirring, putting their heads out of their holes and hollows to welcome the waking day and call to one another in excited greeting.

The venerable oaks that grew between the Hagburn and the cinder track were home to many creatures, but none so singularly strange as the forgotten race of the little werling folk.

How long they had dwelt there, high in the trees, no one knew—for they were accounted small and insignificant and had always been overlooked. Within the richly decorated pages of gold-bound bestiaries, locked deep inside the Hollow Hill, there was no record of their existence. The simple people who practiced the art of wergling were not considered worthy of attention and so had no part in the long, grim histories of that secluded realm. But all that was about to change—the hour of the werlings was fast approaching. Soon even the Most High Lady would be aware of them. This is their tale, and it began upon that bright March morning in a snug chamber within the trunk of a great oak tree.

GRUNTING softly in his sleep, Gamaliel Tumpin lay on his stomach, face buried in the soft, dry moss of the bed. His gentle snores were the pleasant "hums" and "nemyims" of complete contentment, but when his sister barged into that small chamber, shock and annoyance crinkled her face immediately.

"No you don't!" she gasped in outrage. "I won't let you!" And with that she jumped heavily upon the mossy bed. "Idlebones!" she bawled, grabbing her brother's shoulders and shaking him roughly. "Don't you be late this first morning. I doesn't want you making a show of me! Father's bad enough!"

Jolted from sleep, Gamaliel gave a startled cry and was promptly flipped over by his sister's podgy hands.

"How could you doze in today?" she demanded, grabbing a fistful of moss and rubbing it into his unsuspecting face.

Spluttering, Gamaliel pushed her away, but the girl would not be thwarted and, snatching hold of his grubby ankles, hauled him from the bed.

"Kernella!" he squealed. "Let go, let go! I'm awake, I'm awake!"

Casting his struggling feet aside, Kernella Tumpin glowered down at her brother, stern disapproval etched into every freckled furrow of her forehead.

On the floor, spitting out shreds of his nestlike bed, Gamaliel glared back at her.

Kernella was two years older than her brother and took every opportunity to boss and scold him. A plain, plump werling child with short reddish hair that would never hold a curl no matter how hard she tried, she scrutinized the room and voiced her disdain.

"Messier than a rat hole in here." She sniffed, folding her arms in the manner so familiar and annoying to Gamaliel. "You'll not last long if'n you doesn't spruce your ideas up. Master Gibble won't stand for any of your sluggy tats and clutters. Squawk and skreek at you he will, and a good thing it'd be, too, I reckons."

Gamaliel pulled fragments of straw and moss from his gingery hair and waited wearily for his sister to finish.

The arms were still folded and her face set in that belligerent expression that meant she would put up with no nonsense and he had to do precisely as she instructed. It was pointless to argue when she looked like that, even if her two prominent peg-shaped teeth did stick out and make her resemble a vexed rabbit.

"You don't have to stand there," Gamaliel said grumpily. "I can dress myself, you know."

Kernella snorted and eyed the bundles of clothing strewn untidily across the floor. "I'll be shamed to be seen with you," she said, turning on her heel and stomping up the rising passage that led from the chamber. "Don't you go 'specting me to sit next to you neither, for I won't."

"Well that's something, I s'pose." Her brother sighed before making the rudest face he could manage at that early hour.

When she had disappeared from view, he picked himself up from the floor and cast about for his clothes.

Kernella was right: His little room was a mess. The trouble was that Gamaliel could never bear to throw anything away and was always collecting objects he found interesting. His cozy chamber was stuffed with all kinds of bric-a-brac. The niches carved into the curved walls were crammed with these treasures, and the very idea of being parted from any of them made him feel wretched and miserable.

His collection of colorful stones and pebbles had grown so large that they were now heaped all around the room, while his trove of shiny beetles' wings, seeds, and knobbly twigs was beginning to spill out into the passageway. Scattered around the bedside lantern were the fruits of his latest obsession. His father had given him a small knife and Gamaliel had taken up the art of whittling. He had intended to create something so wonderful that it would wipe the superior smirk from his sister's face, but so far he had succeeded in making only an awful lot of wood shavings.

From the ceiling dangled an array of feathers, discovered on his scramblings among the uppermost branches of the oak that the Tumpins shared with two other werling families. Staring up at this dusty hoard, Gamaliel groaned inwardly. When would he have time to go searching for feathers now? Nothing would be the same again.

In dejected silence the young werling hunted through the wreckage of his bed and fished out his jerkin and breeches.

Although he was not as well padded as his sister, Gamaliel Tumpin was of the same plump stature. His face was round and ruddy, and they both possessed bulbous noses. But there the similarities ended. Whereas Kernella was confident and certain of her own skills, Gamaliel was not, and his thoughts were troubled.

Slowly he clambered into his clothes, fastened the belt about his middle, and pulled the warm woolen snookul-hood over his head.

He had been dreading this morning for some time now.

Elsewhere in that quiet region at the edge of Hagwood, the other children his age would be thrilled and excited at the prospect of their very first lesson, but not Gamaliel.

He was certain that he would make a mess of things and do something idiotic. He had never been good at anything, and the recent whittling disappointments were merely the latest in an embarrassing list of failed ventures. Gamaliel was also a clumsy youngster, a fact of which he was painfully aware. When he became flustered or particularly nervous, his awkwardness increased.

"Stop dawdling down there!" his sister suddenly yelled.

Searching for one of his soft leather shoes, Gamaliel stubbed a toe against a favorite pebble and wryly reflected that Kernella was extremely proficient at flustering him.

When the missing shoe was eventually discovered, he

hastily slipped it on, cast a final glance back at the bed, and trudged despondently from the chamber.

Through the gently climbing passage that wound up inside the oak he went, hurrying only when he passed the opening to his sister's lair. At last he came to the main room, where she and their parents were waiting.

"There you are!" Tidubelle Tumpin exclaimed, tapping the table that dominated the family's living space. "Sit you down and have a bite to eat. Got a big day ahead of you. Can't start all that learnin' if you're empty now, can you?"

When she had first married their father, Gamaliel and Kernella's mother had been quite slim, but now she was the correct, round shape for a Tumpin.

Standing at her side, his whiskery face aglow with pride, her husband, Figgle, rocked on his heels and eyed his son affectionately.

"Tendin' Master Gibble's instruction for the first time," he declared. "How well I recall the day I started. His nose weren't as long in them days, but he were still as tetchy. How he worked us. I remember——"

Figgle's wife interrupted him before he could launch into one of his stories. "Tell us later, Tumpin," she said. "I got to give our Gamaliel his present. Go fetch it for us."

"Present!" Figgle repeated in agreement. "Can't do nothin' this day without that." And he hurried over to a corner of the room where a patterned cloth concealed his wife's work baskets.

Already seated at the table and finishing her last nutty mouthful of breakfast, Kernella eyed her father and crossly pushed away her empty bowl.

"Is he never going to get rid of that?" she demanded of her mother. "I know he only keeps it to embarrass me!"

With his head ducked under the cloth, Figgle waggled his bottom from side to side. The bushy red squirrel tail that stuck out incongruously from the seat of his breeches—and so scandalized his daughter—gave a mischievous wave.

"Mother!" Kernella objected. "It's awful. Everyone's laughing at him, and Master Gibble says Father's making a mockery of his teaching."

Withdrawing his head from the cloth, a basket in one hand, Figgle Tumpin gave his tail a consoling pat with the other.

"Nuts and pips!" he told his daughter. "I can grow a tail if I want to. Kept me lovely and warm this winter it has; ever so comfy it is."

Returning to his wife's side, Figgle performed a little jig, and the controversial addition to his posterior traced wide circles in the air behind him.

"'Tis a big help with the dusting," Tidubelle admitted.

"Time for presenting," Figgle announced. He clapped his hands, and the fluffy tail curled almost lovingly about his arm.

Kernella gave it her most withering glare.

Reaching into the basket, Mrs. Tumpin brought out a small black pouch fastened at the neck by two cords, and, with the utmost ceremony, held it out to her son.

"Here, Gamaliel," she said tenderly. "Your special day has finally arrived. At last you will learn the secrets of shape and change—the ancient knowledge that keeps our kind safe and hidden."

Wiping his palms on his jerkin, Gamaliel hesitated before taking the bag from her.

"Your very own wergle pouch," she told him encouragingly. "Made it myself out of the finest mole's skin."

"I caught the mole," Figgle reminded her.

Lifting his gaze from the bag, Gamaliel looked up at his mother and saw the love in her face.

In later years, when he thought about her, it was his mother's smile that first returned to Gamaliel's mind.

Tidubelle had a grin for every occasion. The happiest times were marked with wide displays of teeth—her eyes submerging behind rising cheeks. Lopsided twists of the mouth were reserved for listening to one of their father's many meandering stories; tight-lipped curves were for use at times of reproof; and the rare, soft, shadowy smiles, for moments of sadness. For everyday use she had an all-purpose smile, which suited her the best, and her family never tired of seeing her wear it.

That morning's smile stayed with Gamaliel till the end of his days.

"Thank you," he said as he received the velvety wergle pouch and a kiss on the forehead.

Wiping his nose with the end of his tail, Figgle cleared his throat. "Wear it well, son," he told him. "Never go anywhere without it. Save your life, that will. I know mine has. Before I wed your mother there was this time—"

"I bet he loses it," Kernella said sourly.

Gamaliel scowled at her and secured the pouch to his belt. "Won't," he muttered.

His sister affected a scoffing laugh and fingered her own wergle pouch, which was hung about her neck. Hers was exactly the same as Gamaliel's, except that two red patches had been sewn on to show the levels she had achieved in her training.

"Got a lot of hard work ahead if'n you're goin' to catch up with me," she boasted. "Look what I can do now. Take two years or more to do this, Gamaliel."

Kernella began to forage in her bag, but her mother told her to stop teasing.

"No need to show off," Tidubelle said. "We know how clever you are at it, Kernella. Gamaliel will get there eventually."

The girl shrugged and tied the neck of her wergle pouch again. "No matter how hard Gamaliel tries," she began huffily, "he'll never be as good as Finnen."

"Don't get her started on Finnen Lufkin," Figgle mumbled with a roll of his eyes. "Give our Gamaliel his breakfast."

But there was no time for him to eat anything. At that moment there came the sound of a horn blowing throughout the woodland, and Kernella sprang to her feet.

"Got to go!" she cried, wrapping her cape about her shoulders and scurrying from the room.

"Well," Figgle murmured while his wife stuffed Gamaliel's pockets with food. "This is it, son. That was the summons. You'd best get out there; the others'll be along to take you to Master Gibble. Don't look so worried—just do the best you can."

Taking a deep breath, Gamaliel gave a weak smile, then walked apprehensively down the passage that led to the outside. The moment he had hoped would never arrive was here.

———

AFTER the dim lantern light of the Tumpin home, the late-March sunshine was dazzling, and stepping into it, Gamaliel shielded his squinting eyes.

A warm breeze coursed through Hagwood, and the gently swaying branches played a delightful, rushing music. It was too beautiful a day to commence instruction, and when he gazed out across the leaf canopy, the young werling set his thoughts free.

In all his seven years he had never been allowed to venture anywhere near the banks of the Hagburn, let alone the wilder forest beyond. The children of his race were kept close to home until the wergle training began, but in his dreams he had journeyed far into the dark heart of Hagwood.

Now, one last time, he surveyed that fascinating country of his youthful imaginings and sent his mind traveling: out over the rolling landscape of the treetops to where hushed tales told of gnarled yews that grew so close that not even a ray of light could slip between their tangled branches.

Through that blind gloom he often had pressed, braving hideous perils until at last he arrived at the great green hill—that wonderful spectacle he never tired of gazing upon.

Out over the green rustling sea, that steadfast island reared in the hazy distance, and Gamaliel drank in the vision as he had done countless times before. Of the noble lords and ladies who dwelt within its hallowed halls, there were many bewitching legends, and Gamaliel loved to hear them.

"Perhaps one day...," he whispered to himself, "one day I could go there and see it up close."

At that moment, suddenly and without warning, a fat

squirrel came racing round the oak's great trunk and barged straight into him.

"Hey!" Gamaliel called, flinging his arms wide to keep his balance. But it was no use: His feet slithered from the bark and down he fell.

Into his large ears the air rushed as the tree went shooting by and he tumbled head over heels—plummeting toward the ground.

A startled, gurgling wail accompanied his plunging descent until Gamaliel's instincts took control and his hands reached out to seize hold of a blurring branch. Immediately the breakneck drop came to an abrupt and stomach-jolting halt.

With a rattle of twigs, the branch bowed before springing up again, and the werling was catapulted across the gulf to the trunk. Sweeping his legs high and over, he somersaulted through the distance and landed deftly on the tree—out of breath and angry. The squirrel that had bumped into him had been wearing his sister's cape and hood.

Like all members of the werling race, Gamaliel was an expert at climbing, and he scampered down the oak in a matter of moments.

At the base of the tree, having returned to her own form, Kernella was already waiting. She laughed out loud when she saw how scarlet his face had become.

"Not funny, not funny!" he shouted, jumping onto the sloping ground. "I could have got hurt—killed even!"

"Pooh!" his sister scorned. "I'm sure I doesn't know what you're talking about."

Scooping up a handful of damp leaf mold, Gamaliel hurled it at her, but Kernella leaped aside. She was about to pick up a quantity of the stuff herself when she glanced over her brother's shoulder and thought better of it.

"You two!" a gruff voice called impatiently. "Stop larking about!"

Gamaliel turned sharply, and there, shambling up the gentle bank toward the oak, was a large hedgehog.

"Morning, Mr. Mattock," Kernella said, assuming an air of mock innocence.

The hedgehog shuffled closer. "What are you still doing here, Kernella Tumpin?" the brusque voice demanded.

"Keeping Gamaliel company," the girl promptly fibbed. "Gets horrible scared he does."

Muffled titters issued from the hedgehog's back legs and Gamaliel frowned.

The prickly creature was a sorry-looking specimen: The bulky body sagged in the center and its movements were extremely peculiar. When it drew close to the Tumpin children, the voice called out.

"Halt, back there!"

At once the hedgehog stumbled to a standstill, then its middle drooped even more and it sank strangely to the ground.

Moving closer, Gamaliel peered at the blank holes where the urchin's eyes ought to have been and glimpsed a stern face staring out at him.

"Don't stand there gawping, lad!" the voice chided. "Do you want to be late on your first day? Master Gibble won't like that! Get you in here."

As these words were spoken, the creature's snout gave a violent twitch as if it were about to sneeze. Then its entire head was thrown back, and standing where its face had been was a grave-looking werling dressed in a dark green cloak and with tufts of white bristling hair sprouting from his ears.

This was Yoori Mattock, a much-respected member of the presiding council, but today he, along with four other adults, was collecting those children about to commence their training and conveying them safely to the place of instruction.

Holding the front part of the empty hedgehog skin above his head, he looked at Gamaliel in annoyance.

"Don't gawk, boy!" he snapped. "Do you want a wolf to come along and gobble you up? There's an owl been seen these past few nights. What if it's late getting home and fancies a nibble of your daft head? Death and danger all around—you should know that."

Gamaliel stammered an apology, but his eyes were drawn to the two figures crouching behind Mr. Mattock in the hedgehog's hindquarters. Although they were half hidden in the shade of that prickly camouflage, Gamaliel recognized them, and his heart sank.

Mufus and Bufus Doolan were twins, and because they were the same age as Gamaliel, they, too, were commencing their wergle training that day. Practically identical in appearance, with curly chestnut hair and upturned, usually snotty noses, they shared an irritating snigger and poked fun at everything and everybody.

"Hide and be safe," Mr. Mattock continued. "That's how it's always been. You youngsters can't make your way to Master Gibble's classes on your own. Best disguise, this is, until you're a bit older and have learned a few tricks of your own."

Gamaliel gave the Doolan brothers another uneasy glance. He didn't relish traveling anywhere with them. They were already nudging each other and smirking.

"What ails you, lad?" Mr. Mattock cried. "Get a move on!"

"Yes," Kernella joined in. "Stop dithering!"

Greatly flustered, Gamaliel hastened toward them. But the leaf mold was slippery, and before he knew what was happening, the young werling was flying headfirst down the slope, unable to stop himself.

"Steady!" Mr. Mattock cried.

"Look out!" Kernella shrieked in horror. Unable to witness the mortifying spectacle her idiotic brother was about to make of himself, she hoisted her snookulhood up over her eyes.

In a moment it was over. There was a thump and another, then a bang, followed by a scuffle and squeals from the Doolan brothers, until finally Kernella heard a horrible ripping sound.

"I never did!" came Mr. Mattock's indignant roar. "Never in all my days!"

Anxiously, Kernella lowered her hood and peeped out at the devastation her brother had wrought.

Sprawled on the ground, his face covered in wet leaf mulch, hands thrust bizarrely through the hedgehog's empty ears, Yoori Mattock was fuming. Nearby, Mufus and Bufus were hooting with laughter and pointing down the slope to where Gamaliel was still careering out of control, the back half of the now-torn disguise wrapped tightly around him.

"Gamaliel!" Kernella screeched. "How could you?"

Helpless with mirth, the Doolans gasped for breath and tried to calm themselves, but when the prickly object finally came to rest and a pair of legs wormed their way free, stood up, then fell down again, the twins collapsed anew.

"Don't...don't know about Gamaliel!" Bufus wheezed. "His name should be Gammy."

"Gammy! Gammy! Gammy!" Mufus echoed in rapturous agreement.

Wiping the dirt from his face, Yoori Mattock rose and glared at the ridiculous figure flailing and thrashing on the ground.

"Get over here, you perfect fool!" he raged.

Several minutes later, Gamaliel had managed to clamber out of the spiny binding and was sheepishly ambling back up the slope, dragging it behind him.

Kernella had already fled the scene, not wishing to have anything more to do with him. The bristles of Mr. Mattock's ears were quivering with fury, and the Doolan brothers mocked the poor young werling with the nickname he would bear for a long, long time.

It was not the best of beginnings, but Gamaliel had the uncomfortable feeling that it was going to get a lot worse.

# CHAPTER 2
# The Great Grand Wergle Master

At the foot of a lofty hazel tree, a decidedly ragged and peculiar-looking hedgehog came to rest, and four werlings gladly cast the disheveled and unconvincing deception aside.

It had been a most uncomfortable journey through the wood. Hunched over beneath the damaged skin, Gamaliel had been forced to follow Mr. Mattock as closely as possible and had lost count of the times he stepped upon the elder's heels.

Yoori suffered him in silence, but Gamaliel could sense how angry and exasperated he was. To make matters worse, Mufus and Bufus snickered to themselves the entire time, and on three occasions tried to trip Gamaliel over again.

Because he was in the middle, and because it was his fault anyway, it had been Gamaliel's job to hold the two halves of the hedgehog together, and by the time they reached their destination, Gamaliel's arms were aching and his fingers pricked and sore.

"This is the place," Mr. Mattock informed them, deliberately avoiding Gamaliel's eye. "Looks like everyone else is here. We're late."

Glancing around the tree's roots, the young werlings saw that four other prickly disguises had been abandoned and left until the end of the day, when they would be needed again.

"You'd best climb up there quick as a wink," Mr. Mattock advised. "Master Gibble doesn't like to be kept waiting."

The Doolan brothers needed no further warning and were soon swarming swiftly up the smooth bark of the hazel tree.

"Last one to the top is a Gammy Tumpin!" they called out to each other.

Left behind, Gamaliel turned to Mr. Mattock in an endeavor to make amends, but the agitated werling had already departed, and Kernella's brother caught sight of a green-cloaked stoat darting into a ragged clump of dead ferns.

Shifting his gaze back toward the tree, Gamaliel stared

up at the trunk. "Here we go then," he mumbled to himself.

THE hazel that grew in the peaceful eaves of Hagwood was of immense age and stature. Its lofty branches stretched higher than the surrounding oaks and hornbeams, and since the time when the first werlings settled in that tranquil realm, it had been the place where children were taught to master the marvelous, mysterious art of wergling.

Amid the high branches, a wide platform had been constructed. When Gamaliel Tumpin first peered up through the opening at its center, he saw that he was, indeed, the last youngster to arrive.

Sitting upon that wooden deck were more werling children than he had ever seen assembled together before. At the front, the younger ones could hardly contain their excitement, while behind them their older brothers and sisters were seated upon stools and waiting expectantly.

There were many faces Gamaliel recognized, but some of them were strangers. Concentrating hard, for he was never good at tallying numbers, he counted out a total of thirty-nine.

Kernella was among them, but she was still out of sorts, especially as Gamaliel's behavior had caused her to be late herself, which prevented her from sitting next to the one she never tired of talking about at home.

Nervously her brother glanced around to see if the strict Master Gibble was present and was enormously relieved to discover that he was not. The tutor's familiar black gown was hooked on one of the overhanging branches, but of him as yet there was no sign.

Thankful for this, Gamaliel turned back to the other children and was disconcerted to find that they were all staring at him.

Self-consciously he clambered onto the platform. When she spotted him, Kernella adopted a lofty air, then ignored him completely. Leaning forward, she grinned goofily at a youth several seats away, whose features were hidden by a shaggy fringe.

"Hoo, Finnen!" she called, giving him a bashful wave. "I'll bet you've been practicing all winter, haven't you? Be taking over from Master Gibble himself one of these days, I reckon."

The boy fidgeted uncomfortably and stared at the floor so that the curtain of his long fringe screened his face entirely.

Kernella chortled and eased herself back on the stool. "Might as well give all the prize patches to him right now," she said admiringly. "We know he'll win them, anyway."

At the front of the gathering, Gamaliel was trying to find a place to sit, but there did not appear to be any room. Seeing his predicament, Mufus Doolan budged up a little and shouted.

"Gammy, come sit with us—I dares you. We won't bite."

"I will!" his brother, Bufus, promised.

"N-no." Gamaliel spluttered, feeling foolish in front of everyone. "I don't think…"

His words were drowned out by a sudden squawking cry that croaked and screeched fiercely above their heads.

Glancing upward, the werling children were horrified to see a great magpie come diving through the branches, talons outstretched, its black-and-white wings flapping furiously.

Squeals of terror rang from the hazel tree. The youngsters fell on their faces, throwing their arms over their heads when the savage marauder swooped down, snatching at their hair with its claws.

"We'll be eated!" they screamed shrilly. "Save us! Save us!"

Tumbling from their stools, the older children were whipped by the beating feathers, and for several moments their hearts were filled with panic and despair.

Only two of those present remained where they were. Gamaliel was too thunderstruck and astounded to know what to do, and so throughout all the wild, thrashing frenzy he stood gaping, his green eyes boggling at the frightful spectacle unfolding around him.

The second was Finnen Lufkin. Instead of toppling from his seat as his peers had done, he took an intense interest in the ferocious, shrieking attack. Brushing the hair from his face, he casually chewed his lower lip and stared keenly up at the ravaging bird.

There was something extremely familiar about that lethal-seeming beak. It was far too long for any magpie and was peppered with holes.

"Dab crack," he murmured. "The wily old boaster."

Around him the older children were recovering from their initial shock. Then they began to coo with an amazement that rapidly turned into a peal of fervent applause.

"Hooray!" they cheered. "Isn't he clever? I can't believe it—I really can't."

Aware that the disguise had at last been penetrated, the

26

magpie gave a triumphant croak, then wheeled about the hazel's trunk three times before spreading its wings wide and alighting upon the platform, to the stupefaction of the younger members of the assembly. Lifting their faces from the floor, they looked up at the great bird and marveled.

Shaking its feathers, the magpie paraded up and down, strutting before the astounded gathering. Then, with a conceited look upon its face, it gave a final, jubilant hop, and the feathered form was cast aside.

Effortlessly, the shape of the magpie melted. In a moment the bird had vanished, and in its place was Terser Gibble—the Great Grand Wergle Master.

The tutor of the werlings was one of the most outlandish and extreme examples of their kind. Tall and spindly, his real appearance looked more like a twig than anything else. His aged skin was cracked and lined like the bark of a sycamore, and his long arms were knobbled and skinny.

Taking the black gown from its hook, he wrapped it about himself and, with a flourish, struck an authoritative and ostentatious pose while the children continued to applaud his great skill.

"Amazing!" Kernella cooed. Birds were an incredibly difficult shape to master, and then the art of flying itself was a completely new discipline to overcome. No other werling had succeeded half as well as Master Gibble, and so he deserved the praise lavished upon him.

Still standing at the side, Gamaliel clapped along with everyone else and regarded his new teacher with awe. He knew Terser Gibble by sight, of course—every werling did—but he had never been this close to him before and had never witnessed such a dazzling display of his skill.

Basking in the adoration, the Wergle Master continued posturing and smiled serenely. His face was perhaps the strangest aspect of him. A tuft of wiry hair, like a beard of fibrous roots, projected from the back of his head, but that was perfectly balanced by the longest nose of any werling.

Resembling a blighted, woody parsnip, this nose was his most striking feature. Over the years, many extra nostrils had opened along its prodigious length, and Master Gibble considered it quite splendid. At times of temper or high indignation, his snorting breath would blast from those holes in sharp whistling notes. The effect was quite startling and commanded him much respect both from his students and from the rest of the werling community.

When the applause subsided, the gangly tutor gave an extravagant bow, but even as he gracefully inclined his head, his small black eyes fell upon Gamaliel and at once he jerked to attention.

"You there!" his pinched voice barked. "What ails your knees?"

Alarmed and bewildered by the question, Gamaliel stuttered. "N-nothing, sir."

"Then use them and sit down!" Master Gibble snapped back.

Gamaliel shivered as if stung. The tutor petrified him, but he was now too shaken to do anything and remained standing like a dummy.

"I said sit!" Master Gibble repeated, and this time his voice was full of command.

But Gamaliel could only stare back at him, and an absurd burble issued from his trembling lips. Behind him Mufus and Bufus started to titter.

"What's your name?" the Wergle Master demanded, jabbing the air with a sticklike finger. "Whose idiot child are you? Speak now, speak!"

Gamaliel shook his head dumbly and wished he had never woken up that morning.

"He's called Gammy," Bufus piped up. "He's barmy."

"A clot!" his brother added.

At the back of the assembly, Kernella disowned Gamaliel completely and became suddenly fascinated by the branches above her head.

Displeasure flared three of Master Gibble's nostrils, and a soft hiss, like the sound of a kettle just before it comes to the boil, emanated from them.

"Clot, indeed." He seethed, pursing his lips and taking a menacing stride toward Gamaliel. "If I am expected to squander my genius instructing imbeciles, then they must at least know how to obey. If the dolt does not seat himself before I get to him, I shall snatch him up and hurl him over the edge."

Watching the tutor take a second purposeful step in his direction, Gamaliel felt his eyes begin to tingle and knew that he was about to cry.

Master Gibble was almost upon him when a delicate hand reached up and tugged at Gamaliel's sleeve.

"Here!" a kindly voice began. "I've made a space; sit next to me."

A further tug was all that was needed for Gamaliel's legs to give way beneath him, and he plopped down on the deck with a bump.

"Th-thank you," he managed to utter to the pretty werling girl who had saved him.

Master Gibble sneered and scrutinized his plump face for a moment.

"Now I see it," he began acidly. "You're a Tumpin, aren't you? Well, that explains a great deal. Your father was a pupil of mine. He was an idle dreamer then and has since become a disgrace to all. If I had my way, I should exile him, send him out over the Hagburn and let him fend for himself against the terrors of the great forest. With that ludicrous tail of his, he has brought my noble teachings down to the lowest possible level. To hide from the eyes and minds of our enemies, that is the sole purpose of our art. It is not to keep our toes warm!"

Still contemplating the branches, Kernella was not simply an only child but she promptly orphaned herself as well.

"Whatever next?" the tutor continued as he turned from Gamaliel and moved back to the center of the platform. "Shall we grow rabbits' tails to serve as cushions? Instead of hats we could all develop snail shells upon our heads, or keep long weasel bodies if we consider our natural stature too diminutive."

Clasping his hands, he faced his audience and in a grave, somber voice warned, "If we debase our gift, then we debase ourselves, and only tragedy will follow."

In the ensuing silence, the children nodded their agreement, but Finnen Lufkin stared long at Master Gibble until his fringe fell back across his face.

Swinging his nose from side to side, the Great Grand Wergle Master appraised his new pupils and sniffed. It was time.

Flinging his arms wide so that the black gown billowed impressively about him, he cleared his throat and blew a short, shrill blast from his nostrils.

The instruction commenced.

ᎤNLIKE other inhabitants of Hagwood, the forgotten race of werlings possessed only one grain of magic. But that single, simple blessing had preserved their way of life for untold ages.

The miraculous power of transformation, or "wergling" to give it the proper name, was theirs to command. They had the ability to change their shape at will and become any creature of a similar size to themselves. Yet before this talent could be used, there were many teachings to study and rules to be learned. To embark upon any change of shape without the correct instruction was unheard of and undoubtedly dangerous, so there was always a Wergle Master present whose role was to guide and educate the novices.

Terser Gibble was the latest in a distinguished line of respectable tutors, but few had ever gloried in such a skill as his. For three generations he had overseen the development of the charges in his care, and he was the most important personage in the entire community.

"The first and most important lesson to learn," he began, "is to know the ways of the beast whose shape you desire to assume. You cannot become another creature if you are ignorant of its habits."

Clicking his bony fingers, he looked at his older students. "How do we go about this?" he asked them.

Kernella thrust her hand in the air, but he was not predisposed to have any more dealings with the base Tumpin clan that day and chose another eager hand, instead.

"Learn all you can about the animal," a girl named Stookie Maffin chirped. "We must think like it before we can look like it."

"Sloppily put," Master Gibble pouted. "But that is the essence, I suppose."

Returning his gaze to Gamaliel's class, he continued. "You will train your minds to step beyond their current boundaries and limitations to embrace all that you can become. As Mistress Maffin so ineloquently related, first you must study the beast, run with it, and know its habits. Only when you understand its spirit can you wear its external appearance."

With a click of his tongue, Master Gibble then announced that the best time to begin this most important aspect of the training was straight away.

"Bearing everything I have said in mind, you shall spend the rest of the day pursuing and studying the creature that is the simplest to wergle into—the least complicated of all animals from our point of view. Do any of you know which lowly animal I mean?"

Mufus Doolan was about to suggest a "Gammy," but someone else called out the answer before he had a chance.

"Please, sir," a high voice cried. "Would it be a mouse?"

Master Gibble clapped his hands. "It is, indeed," he said. "The mouse is the creature shape that we all learn first, so that is what you shall do today. I want each of you to hunt one down, for during the chase you shall discover much. Now, does everyone have their wergle pouches ready? Good, because in those I want you to place a handful of the mouse's fur. I cannot stress how important that is. Needless to say, you will not be able to do any wergling without it."

And so the children were divided into smaller groups. Gamaliel found himself placed with the girl who had rescued him from Master Gibble's wrath. Her name was Liffidia. The other members of his group were a small boy named Tollychook (whose nose showed all the signs that one day it might rival that of Master Gibble) and, to his dismay, the Doolan brothers.

Each party was joined by an older child who would oversee their efforts and ensure that they came to no harm during the hunt. Gamaliel prayed that he would not be burdened with Kernella, but when he discovered that none other than Finnen Lufkin was to be their guide, he was filled with misgivings.

To all of the children Finnen Lufkin was a hero. In the two years since his training began, he had excelled at everything. The Lufkin family had always been champions of the art, but Finnen's skill surprised even Terser Gibble. It was rumored that he didn't need to use his wergle pouch anymore. Confronted with his sister's idol, Gamaliel felt uncomfortable and was sure he would look even more foolish in comparison.

Finnen grinned at the five children. "Hello," he said. Then, with a friendly nod at Gamaliel, "So you're Kernella's brother. Don't let old Gibble put the wind up you. There's nothing to worry about; it's not as difficult as it sounds."

Gamaliel managed a feeble smile. That was easy for someone with Finnen's remarkable reputation to say.

Once every group had been allocated a leader, they were

instructed to make their way down the tree. When they were all gathered about the roots, Master Gibble addressed them again.

"The moment I give the signal," he said, lifting his left hand above his head in readiness, "I want you to run into the wood, but remain in your groups—no scattering or wandering off on your own."

The boy called Tollychook stared at the surrounding woodland, then looked down at the empty hedgehog disguises.

"Ain't we usin' them then?" he asked worriedly. "I'm afeared of being summat's dinner."

Master Gibble pursed his lips. "That camouflage is for conveying you here in the morning and taking you home in the evening," he answered tartly. "You'll never catch a mouse while wearing one of those. I'm not saying that your allotted task is without an element of danger, but there is no other way. Besides, the peril will sharpen your senses."

Tollychook grimaced and sucked his teeth unhappily. "I doesn't like it," he warbled.

"You'll be all right," Finnen whispered reassuringly. "I'll be there to make sure you're safe."

The boy brightened a little, but the wood was awfully big and threatening.

"Enough!" Master Gibble declared. "Let the hunt commence."

Down swept his arm, and sitting high in the branches above them, one of the older pupils who had remained behind put a small horn to her lips and blew a loud blast upon it.

Immediately the separate groups of children ran from the hazel tree. Squealing with exhilarated glee, they charged off in different directions, haring in the footsteps of their leaders.

The first adventure had begun.

# CHAPTER 3
# Hunting and Finding

This way!" Finnen called, racing through a clump of dead stalks. "I know the perfect spot where there'll be hundreds of mice. We'll be back before you know it."

To make the hunt easier for the children, many of the adult werlings were hidden throughout the wood. It was their job to act as beaters, driving mice from their holes and out into the open. When the adults heard the blowing of the horn, they set about their work with sticks and cudgels. A fearsome din erupted in the undergrowth.

Over twisting roots and under fallen branches, Finnen Lufkin's little party hurried. The Doolans kept up with Finnen easily, and Liffidia was close behind them. A little further back, Tollychook continuously switched his gaze from the way ahead to the sky above—just in case a kestrel had strayed from the heath and was hovering up there, waiting to pounce upon him. Bringing up the rear, Gamaliel Tumpin huffed and panted. His tubby figure was not made for running along the woodland floor, and he hoped that they would not have much farther to go.

Ahead of him, the others suddenly dived through a hedge of elder. Feeling horribly alone, Gamaliel spurred himself forward with as much speed as he could muster.

Into the gloom that lay beneath the elder he plunged, then out into the bright sunlight again, and there he stumbled to a halt, staring delightedly about him.

Gamaliel was standing on a mossy bank, looking down into a small clearing filled with short grasses and the brown stems of last year's flowers. Liffidia, Mufus, Bufus, and Tollychook were close by; they, too, could not believe their eyes. Seeing their astonished faces, Finnen chuckled.

"I told you I knew the best place," he said.

His eyes round with wonderment, Tollychook slapped his cheeks and gurgled in disbelief.

"Glory me!" he trilled. "Look at that—just look. Glory me!"

Liffidia gasped and covered her mouth with her hands, shaking her head so much that one of the wooden beads that were threaded into her hair flew off and hit Mufus on the back of the head. The spectacle before them was incredible, and even the Doolan brothers were momentarily lost for words.

The glade that Finnen Lufkin had led them to was swarming with mice.

Driven from their homes by the beaters, it seemed that every mouse west of the Hagburn had poured into this clearing in their panicking flight. There were so many of them that the grass writhed and the brittle canes of the dead flowers shuddered, their parched leaves trembling and the seed heads rattling. The place was alive with rustling movement and the piercing sound of confused squeaks and squeals.

"Don't just stand there!" Finnen laughed at his charges. "They're only dashing through. Go catch one."

Roused from stupefaction, the children gave a shout and went scrambling down the bank, diving into the grass as though it were a deep pool.

After the stampeding hordes they sped, rampaging along channels already made by the streaming rodents. At first, Bufus and Mufus were too busy acting the fools to be of any use whatsoever. Pulling fearful faces at the startled creatures, they yelled and hollered but were so busy giggling that the mice easily darted away from them.

Poor Tollychook, as well as owning a long nose, also possessed large, wide feet, and he made such a trampling that no mouse ventured near him at all.

"Here, little twitchers!" he called, to no avail. "Don't go that way! Come back!"

Gamaliel also was finding it far more difficult than he had supposed. Whereas his blundering did not make such a din as Tollychook and he actually saw many mice bolt by, catching hold of them was another matter entirely.

They moved like lightning. Just when he fixed a brown whiskery face in his sights, in a twinkling it veered instantly aside. If he lunged forward to grab at a pink tail, his hands would grasp only empty air. Gamaliel began to suspect that he was simply too slow, but he tried not to let the thought discourage him and threw himself into the hunt all the more.

Liffidia was far more successful than any of them. Making her way to the center of the glade, she leaped and danced while the rodents coursed around her. Sometimes she ran alongside them, speaking with gentle words. The werling girl loved reaching out to stroke a furry back or tickle a silken ear. Not once did she try to catch one, and from his vantage point upon the bank, Finnen watched her with concern.

"Of course," he murmured to himself, "at the moment it's just a grand game to them. They don't really understand yet."

Mufus and Bufus were enjoying themselves so much that they didn't want the chase to end. When they grew bored of scaring the hapless mice, they began harrying them in earnest. Storming through the grass, they rushed after the squeaking quarry, bawling threats and praising the pleasures of mouse stew.

The Doolan brothers were so swift and worked so well together that they soon gave an exultant cheer. Crowing and whooping, they raised their hands to flaunt an unfortunate victim dangling from their fingers.

Wriggling in terror, the small mouse cried pitifully and hid its face in its paws.

"Skweee! Skweee!" Bufus baited, swinging the creature by the scruff.

His brother sniggered, then regarded the catch with dissatisfaction. "'Tis only a tidgey one," he grumbled. "Us can do better'n that tiddler."

"Righto!" Bufus agreed, and he flung the astonished mouse back into the grass.

Their confidence in their abilities was supreme, and they began the hunt all over again.

Observing them, Finnen tutted. "Somehow I don't think we'll be the first ones back to the hazel after all." He sighed.

In the glade, the youngsters continued the pursuit, and quickly they began to anticipate the rodents' nimble movements. To compensate for his heavy footfalls, Tollychook learned to mimic the frantic squeals and lured many of them toward him, only to be thwarted at the last instant when they saw their mistake and fled.

Liffidia was still happily bounding alongside them. At the far edge of the clearing were numerous bolt-holes, into which many of the mice would disappear, and sometimes she scooted in after them. Down unlit tunnels she ventured, the squeals echoing eerily around her. Through that pitch-dark maze the slender werling girl ran until the passage began to rise and she emerged in a tangle of tree roots, then out into the sweet fresh air once more.

When they saw what she was doing, the Doolan brothers did the same. Into the holes they pelted and were so impressed by the echoes that they screamed and howled at each other throughout the length of their underground journeying.

Upon the bank, even Finnen could hear their racketing

progress below the soil. He knew that valuable lessons were being learned; the minds and lives of mice were being discovered. However, he felt that the time had come for the tokens to be claimed.

When Mufus and Bufus next appeared, grimy but grinning from their subterranean riots, he told them they had to concentrate on the task that Master Gibble had set. Still shouting, the twins darted back into the grass.

Irritated by his failure thus far and seeing no other way around the problem, Tollychook had an idea. Marching up to one of the dead stalks, he snapped it free and tested its strength.

Content with the new rattling weapon, his face set and resolute, he tramped noisily to the nearest mouse run and waited.

"Haha!" Mufus cried abruptly.

"Hoohoo!" Bufus shrieked an instant later.

Simultaneously, both boys lifted a frightened mouse above their heads, and before the unhappy animals could squeal in protest, they each seized hold of a handful of fur and gave a hard, sharp yank.

A duet of pain erupted from their victims, but the tokens had been won and the Doolans set the mice free, waving their trophies proudly and bursting into a boastful song.

"Well done!" Finnen called. "Now bind the fur tightly and put it inside your pouches."

While the brothers obeyed, Finnen scanned the glade for Liffidia. The werling girl had still made no effort to capture a mouse, and seeing her capering joyously amid the teeming rodents, he knew that she was never going to.

Rolling up his sleeves, Finnen Lufkin jumped from the

bank and hastened through the grass until he was standing at Liffidia's side.

"What are you doing?" he demanded. "You've had plenty of chances."

Liffidia smiled at him gravely. "Do you really want me to trap one of these lovely creatures?" she asked.

"That's what old Gibble's told you to do!" he replied. "That's why we're here!"

The girl shrugged and glanced briefly about her. "Very well," she said, and springing forward, Liffidia wrapped her arms about a fleeing mouse's neck. With consummate ease she landed the animal and patted its head to quell its fear.

"Excellent!" Finnen exclaimed in admiration. "Now pull a clump of fur out."

Liffidia stared at him with her large gray eyes. "I'll do no such thing," she retorted. "It's cruel."

"But you have to!" Finnen insisted. "It doesn't do the mouse any harm."

"How would you like it if I pulled your hair out?" she demanded.

"That's different."

"No, it's not."

"All right, all right. So it'll hurt a bit, but think of what old Gibble will say."

Liffidia laughed. "I don't care about that," she said. Then, kissing the mouse's nose, she let it go, and the creature sped away.

The older boy looked at her in astonishment. "You really don't care, do you?" he muttered.

"Did you on your first day?" she asked.

Finnen nodded. "More than anything."

Liffidia thought she heard a profound sadness in his voice, but she was not able to ponder the reason for long.

Poised for action, with the dead stalk as his weapon, Tollychook finally got his chance. From the grass in front of him a mouse's head appeared. For several moments they stared at each other, frozen with alarm—surprise registering upon both their faces.

"Got you!" Tollychook finally cried, but before he could bring the broken stem crashing down, the mouse turned tail.

"No you don't!" Tollychook shouted, lumbering after it and waving the stalk before him.

Frantically he struck out, bashing the ground and missing the mouse, until at last he managed to whack it sideways and the creature was sent spinning across the glade.

Gleefully Tollychook threw his stem away and scooped up the mouse before it could recover.

"Got you, I got you!" he cried, hugging the struggling prize to his chest and almost suffocating it. "Oh, my pretty squeaker, don't fight so. I only wants a snippet of your coat now."

Capturing a mouse was one thing, but Tollychook discovered that holding on to it was even more troublesome. The wretched beast would not keep still. Every time he tried to grab a handful of fur, a leg would kick or the tail would lash across his face. Wrestling with it, he at last seized hold of a fair-sized fistful of soft, sleek hair and pulled.

The mouse squealed, but then so did Tollychook, for even as the fur tore free, the rodent twisted about and bit his nose. Howling, the boy dropped both his attacker and his trophy.

When Finnen arrived to see what had happened, Tolly-chook was hopping about and holding his nose.

Finnen groaned. The hunt had not turned out the way he had hoped. Only Gamaliel was left now, and Finnen went in search of him.

Kernella's brother was exhausted. He had chased every mouse he had seen but had not touched so much as a tail tip, and was now far too tired to go running after them.

Doubled over, he puffed and wheezed—his face almost beetroot in color.

Viewing him from the bank, Mufus and Bufus heckled and scoffed.

"Gammy can't even catch his breath!" they hooted.

Doing his best to ignore them, Gamaliel was determined to try again. Yet the number of mice scurrying through the clearing was dwindling. Most of those driven out by the beaters already had passed into the wood in search of safer havens, and when he realized this, Gamaliel was afraid that he would never catch one.

Anxiously he hurried to and fro as the last stragglers skittered into the glade, but it was no use. He was far too slow and kept tripping.

The Doolan brothers considered this to be the best part of the day so far and threw themselves onto the moss in tearful hysterics.

"I can't bear it no more!" Mufus wept. "I'll bust."

"There's another one!" Bufus commentated. "Gammy's lurchin'—no, he missed it. He's fell down again. He's not getting up—he's conked out!"

For the umpteenth time that day, Gamaliel Tumpin lay

facedown on the ground. It was finally too much, and he burst into tears.

"I can't do it!" he sobbed. "I'm no good for anything. I'm useless."

Coming to kneel beside him, Finnen waited for the anguish to ebb a little before saying anything.

"Wipe your eyes," he said gently. "I'll help you. Follow me."

Sniffling into the neck of his snookulhood, Gamaliel rose. "W-where we going?" he asked.

Finnen smiled but said nothing, and waving to the others to remain where they were, he led Gamaliel from the clearing.

Ascending the opposite bank, the two of them pressed into the wide woodland beyond. Drying his tears, Gamaliel could not begin to guess where he was being taken. But he did not have to wonder for very much longer. A fallen tree stretched across their path, and the older boy halted.

Hesitantly, Gamaliel stared up at the massive obstacle. The tree was overgrown with ivy, and bright orange fungi ballooned from the sweet-smelling wood.

Stepping up to the rotting giant, Finnen held out his hand and ran his fingers over the ivy's dark leaves.

"In here," he muttered.

Pulling the trailing growth aside, he peered into the shade, and Gamaliel did the same.

Revealed beneath the evergreen curtain was an opening in the fallen trunk, large enough for a werling to clamber inside. Before they entered, Finnen put a finger to his lips and whispered.

"Don't make a sound and say nothing."

With that he ducked under the leaves, and Gamaliel followed him in.

To his surprise it was not completely dark within the dead tree. A dim gray light filtered from the opening they had just crawled through, and the sloped ceiling was pricked with many beetle-chewed holes. Nevertheless, it took a little while before Gamaliel's eyes became accustomed to the sudden change.

Directly in front of him, Finnen was treading carefully forward, moving gradually deeper into the tree, and remembering his command, Gamaliel held back his questions and stole after him in silence.

"Gently now," Finnen murmured. "You know me. Peace, old one."

Puzzled, for the older boy was not addressing him, Gamaliel stood on tiptoe and peered over Finnen's shoulder.

He gasped sharply. At the far end of the hollow space a pair of eyes was shining at them.

There came an agitated rustling, and Finnen spoke soothingly.

"Hush, now," he said, approaching those glittering points. "No reason to be afraid. 'Tis only Finnen, your friend."

The nervous movements continued, and Gamaliel finally saw the creature's shape emerge from the shadows that gathered about its nest of dead leaves.

It was a mouse, but the oldest mouse that he had ever seen. The fur was gray, brindled with white, and the whiskers had fallen from its face. One of the papery ears was torn, and as he drew closer, Gamaliel saw that the eyes were almost blind.

"There we are," Finnen breathed as he held out his hand and the wrinkled nose gave a fearful sniff. "Now you know, don't you?"

Reaching up, he caressed the aged animal's head and it nuzzled into his palm.

Enthralled, Gamaliel held his breath to prevent himself from making any noise. It was obvious that the mouse's trust in Finnen was absolute, but he could not imagine how this unusual friendship had developed. Resting its head against the older boy's chest, the mouse murmured a low rumble of content.

"Too old to run with the others, weren't you?" Finnen murmured. "Same as you were back then, when I first found you."

A shriveled paw dabbed at the air, and the boy chuckled warmly.

"Not much today," he admitted, opening a leather bag attached to his belt. "Just some dried apple pieces."

They seemed more than acceptable, and chattering quietly to itself, the mouse waited until the preserves were offered before taking them in its paws. Yet it did not eat them. Instead, the mouse gazed up at Finnen with its milky eyes, and the werling smiled lovingly.

At that moment, Gamaliel found that he could hold his breath no longer and exhaled with a loud "Paaahhh!"

The mouse shuddered and blinked at him, suddenly aware of his presence.

"It's all right," Finnen assured it. "This is another friend of mine."

The half-blind eyes turned back to Finnen, and a look of understanding passed between them.

Placing the morsels of food on the floor, the old creature eased itself wearily down on its side and rolled over. It knew what was needed, and it settled itself into the nest, closed its eyes, and waited.

Finnen beckoned to Gamaliel. "Here," he said. "Take a handful of fur from its back. It won't struggle or run away."

Gamaliel shambled forward. Why was the creature allowing him to do this?

Stretching out his hand, he reached for the hoary gray back, but hesitated when he noticed something that intrigued him. Just below the mouse's shoulders was a bare patch of mottled skin. A few of the hairs had grown back, but the rodent was so ancient that most of the area had remained bald. What had happened? Had someone else removed a scrap of fur? Is that why the animal knew what was required of it?

Gamaliel glanced at Finnen, but the boy avoided his gaze. "Quickly," he told him.

Twining his fingers in the white fur, Gamaliel pulled as gently as he was able.

The mouse trembled beneath him and gave a forlorn whimper when the hairs were extracted.

"There now," Finnen crooned, falling to his knees and cupping the creature's face in his hands. "It's over. You have been so brave. Bless you."

Staring at the clump of snowy fur in his grasp, Gamaliel shifted awkwardly. "Yes," he began, not knowing what else to say. "Thank you."

He was not sure if the mouse heard him, for Finnen was stroking its nose and whispering into the ragged ear.

"Rest now," he told it. "I'll come back, you know that."

Into a dark corner of its nest the mouse retreated, its milky eyes fixed devotedly upon Finnen.

The hero of the werling children raised his hand in farewell and led Gamaliel from the fallen tree.

"We must return to the others," he said. "It's getting late; time we got back to the hazel."

As they made their way to the clearing, Gamaliel reflected on all that had happened. He had failed the first lesson, but at least he would not have to face Master Gibble with an empty wergle pouch. That was solely because of Finnen, and Gamaliel was extremely grateful. There was much more to Master Lufkin than he had suspected, but such ponderings would have to wait, for he was already worrying about what would happen when they reached the hazel tree. The next step in the training would be the most difficult of all—Gamaliel would have to wergle for the very first time.

*What if I'm no good at that, either?* he thought unhappily.

# CHAPTER 4
# The Rules of Wergling

Midday had come and gone by the time Finnen's group rejoined the other werlings upon the platform. They were the last ones back, but the rest were too busy telling one another of their exploits to notice.

Kernella, however, had been keeping a special vigil for their return, and when she saw Finnen arrive she pushed her way through the excited throng to greet him.

"Ooh, Finnen!" she exclaimed teasingly. "Where you been all this time? Gettin' fair worried I was, nearly sent out a search party. Not like you, it ain't."

Finnen gave her a half smile but offered no explanation; it was Mufus Doolan who did that.

"We would've been back ages ago!" he shouted. "If it hadn't been for Gammy—great stupid lump he is. Wasted hours waitin' for him."

The pleasure died on Kernella's face, and she pulled such a grisly expression that both Doolans scurried quickly away.

Miserable, Gamaliel was about to shuffle off into a corner when Finnen stopped him.

"I know exactly how you feel," he said. "You're terrified that you'll make more mistakes and that everyone will laugh."

"'Course I am," Gamaliel answered.

"It's only the first day," Finnen continued, trying to restore the boy's confidence. "When I started wergling I was absolutely terrible at it. I wanted to die—I really did."

"You?" Gamaliel asked in amazement. "But you're the best. Kernella's always saying so."

Finnen sighed. "Not at the beginning I wasn't. Nobody remembers that now, but I do."

Before he could say any more, Terser Gibble waded into the assembly, waving his twiggy arms and calling for attention.

"I see that we are all returned," his clipped voice cried. "I trust there were no mishaps. No one's head has been bitten off and no gizzards are pecked out? Good, then what is the reason for this inane yikkering? Stop it at once."

The talk ceased immediately.

Master Gibble pressed his lips together and roved his black gleaming eyes across their expectant faces.

"So," he announced. "You now know what it is to run with a mouse in the wood."

Every young head nodded vigorously.

"That is as it should be," he said in solemn tones. "You have run and you have hunted. The first step upon the path of wisdom has been taken. Each of you has accomplished the task I set. You have plucked out enough fur to serve as a token so that your experience will not be forgotten."

Again the heads wagged—except for Liffidia's.

The eyes of Master Gibble arrested their roaming, and a sharp glint stabbed out at her.

"You, child!" he snapped abruptly. "What's your name?"

"Liffidia Nefyn," she replied, raising her head and returning his stare as squarely as she was able.

A corner of the tutor's mouth twitched, and his dark brows knitted tightly together. "The daughter of Miwalen and Aikin," he muttered, considering her with distaste. "Your mother was a willful and headstrong pupil; is it so with you? Tell me, child, did you obey my instruction and bring a token of mouse fur back with you?"

An ominous silence fell as he waited for the answer.

"She's in for it now," Finnen whispered to Gamaliel. "I tried to warn her."

Clearing her throat, Liffidia took a deep breath and in a clear, level voice said, "No, I did not."

The effect on Master Gibble was alarming. With every nostril flaring, he strode through the ranks and seized the girl by the shoulders.

"Explain!" he demanded.

Liffidia frowned back at him. "It's cruel!" she cried. "I

won't pull the fur out of any living creature. If that's what it takes to wergle, then I don't want to be trained at all!"

A shocked murmur sprang from the children around her, and Master Gibble's face trembled with rage.

"You don't want to be trained," he repeated, his voice straining to remain calm. "She doesn't want to be trained!"

Twirling about so that his black gown flowed wildly around him like a sloshing puddle of ink, he gave a snort of exasperation, then rounded on her again.

"Just how do you imagine you will survive?" he spat with a hiss. "Without this most vital of skills, you will be vulnerable to all predators. Do you wish to be carried off by a hawk? Is that not what happened to Aikin, your father? Was he not snatched from the wood two summers since?"

Liffidia lowered her eyes. "Why can't I just learn to become a butterfly or a dragonfly, instead?" she asked unhappily.

At those words a gasp of horror issued from the mouths of the others, and the youngsters closest to her moved away.

"Oh, no," Finnen breathed. "How can she not know?"

Gamaliel bit his lip nervously. Even he realized the dreadful mistake she had just made, and his heart went out to the poor, ignorant werling girl.

"A butterfly!" Terser Gibble shrieked, throwing his hands in the air and gesticulating madly. "A butterfly! A dragonfly!"

Dragging his knobbly fingers over his barklike scalp, then down his long nose, he struggled to control himself.

"How dare you harbor such desires, child!" he rasped. "Did your mother never tell you?"

Staring at the floor in great discomfort, Liffidia slowly

shook her head. "I don't understand," she replied in a small voice. "What's so wrong in that?"

The tutor's nostrils quivered and began to make a fizzing sound. "One of the most important and basic rules of wergling," he cried, holding his head in his hands as if it were close to bursting, "is to know what is and is not permitted. Liffidia Nefyn, if you have been deaf these seven years, then unclog your ears this very moment and hearken to me. The insect world is denied to us. It is strictly forbidden! We must never, under any circumstance, be tempted to assume their form. Do you understand? Surely you have heard of Frighty Aggie?"

"I thought that was just a cradle story," she mumbled. "A make-believe monster to frighten the young."

A discordant note whistled from Master Gibble's nose as he hunched over to bring his face close to hers, and he chanted a rhyme that was known to every werling:

> "Crickle crackle, wergle thee,
> Stray not from the cobweb tree.
> Catch my brother or eat my mother,
> O Frighty Aggie, sting not me.

"Would that she were only a nursery bogey," he uttered darkly. "But she is not. The horror that is Frighty Aggie is as real as you or I. Doubt that at your peril, child. Beyond the Hagburn she dwells, devouring what she finds in the darkness. Pray that she never returns to her old haunts, to climb our trees and reach into our homes. What chance would you stand then, against such a nightmare as she, you with no shape but your own to wear?"

Liffidia swallowed dismally. "I'm sorry," she said.

Master Gibble drew himself up. "O Frighty Aggie, sting not me," he echoed. "The next time you yearn to be an insect, remember those words and shun such forbidden wishes."

Spinning upon the bony heels of his bare feet, he marched back to the front and commanded Liffidia to follow.

"As you have no token, you cannot take part in this," he informed her. "Remain there and watch the progress of your fellows. You will have to catch up later."

And so Liffidia was compelled to stand before the other children while Master Gibble turned his back on her and instructed them in the noble art of wergling.

"Now," he began brusquely, "let us resume our journey on the path of wisdom. This very day you will attempt your very first change of form. This is a gift we are born with, but for the novice there are many dangers. Most hazardous of all is to assume a shape but be unable to return to your own. Does anyone know how we defend ourselves against this hideous risk?"

Many hands shot up. "The passwords!" came the children's eager cries. "The passwords."

Master Gibble clicked his tongue and waited for silence. "Many years ago," he proclaimed, when they had settled down once more, "our ancestors devised words of power."

Even as he said it a thrill ran through his audience. The passwords were the werlings' most guarded secret. No one outside their race knew them; to speak of their existence to any stranger was a most heinous offense. Children were not told them until the day of instruction, and during the past two years Kernella often had taunted Gamaliel because she knew and he did not.

Terser Gibble narrowed his eyes and his voice became even more grave than ever.

"Words of power," he continued, "that could unlock whatever form they had taken. If you are in difficulty then these mighty words will save you. They can also be invoked to aid any other of our kind should they be trapped in a shape and unable to break free themselves. Whatever happens, the passwords must not be used frivolously or shouted aloud, lest enemies overhear."

The last sentence was spoken with such severity that one child appeared on the verge of tears, but the point had been driven home, and the Wergle Master was satisfied by the fearful expressions graven upon his pupils' faces.

Moving forward, he pushed into their midst, and when he next spoke it was in a hushed, reverential whisper.

"Heed then," he began, turning this way and that to ensure no other creatures were within earshot. "I shall tell to you the words of power and you must commit them to the innermost regions of your heart."

In silent rapture, the werling youngsters clambered around him and listened intently.

> "*Amwin par cavirrien sul, olgun forweth, i rakundor.*
> *Skarta nen skila cheen,*
> *Emar werta i fimmun-lo.*
> *Perrun lanssa dirifeen, tatha titha Dunwrach.*"

The children uttered small exclamations of dismay.

"I won't never 'member all them tongue tanglers," Tollychook moaned, giving voice to their concerns. "If'n my werglin' goes wrong, I reckons I'm stuck."

Master Gibble regarded him haughtily. "They were cre-
ated in the old speech," he said. "And handed down from
our beginnings. In that form they possess the greatest
strength, yet there is a loose translation that may be easier for
you to learn. It will be all you need at this stage of your instruction. The beasts that you wergle into will be the most
rudimentary, so the simple version will suffice for now."

Again he adopted the low, respectful tone, and the
young werlings listened a second time.

"I call on ye who lay beneath, soil and sky, bark
    and leaf.
Unyoke flesh, unbar door,
Cast off shape and wear no more.
Give again the form that's good, by the might of
    great Hagwood."

"'At's better!" Tollychook cried. "'Unyoke flesh, unbar
door.' Tain't so tricky, thatun."

Master Gibble scowled, and his bony hand flashed out
to smack Tollychook soundly across the back of the head.

"Idiot child!" he raged. "Do you want the world to
hear? Speak not so loudly if you have to utter those words
at all."

Rubbing his smarting head, Tollychook mumbled an
apology.

"And so the moment has come," Master Gibble announced to the rest. "Remove from your wergle pouches the
tufts of fur you have brought from the wood."

Gamaliel reached into his velvety bag and took out the
snowy fur. He was so nervous that he could feel his heart

beating rapidly in his chest, and a tear of perspiration trickled down his forehead. Glancing sideways to where the older children were watching, he saw Finnen grin encouragingly across at him.

"Attention everyone!" Terser Gibble declared. "You must recall what it was like to run with the beast you have hunted this day. Let your mind return to the chase, fill your thoughts with that creature and concentrate on its form. Think so hard that your head hurts. Believe that you are mice."

Pausing a moment to observe the captivated faces of his audience, the tutor then added, "Some of you may find it helpful to imitate a mouse's voice at that point. Of course, there are those who prefer to chant a favorite word over and over to themselves. So long as it aids the illusion and directs the mind I don't care what it is. I recall one pupil who could never wergle into anything until he had recited 'chunky chestnut clusters' thirty times. Then, when your imagination can do no more, take that handful of fur and hold it under your noses to take a great, inspiring whiff. As the smell and nature of the beast fills your nostrils, strain with all your might."

Master Gibble ended with a theatrical sweep of his hands, and the children were ready.

"Begin!" he commanded.

Eagerly the young werlings closed their eyes and everyone thought back to the hunt, recalling as much as they could. In their minds they pictured those brown furry faces and heard the frightened squeals again. A few of the children began to squeak in anticipation, while others muttered under their breath.

Viewing them critically, Master Gibble saw a crowd of crinkled foreheads as each youngster struggled and strained. He grunted approvingly; this was how it should be. They were all endeavoring to overcome the boundaries of their present form.

*Just a little longer,* he told himself.

Outside the gathering, Finnen Lufkin felt the atmosphere intensify. But as he stared at those reddening faces, watching the effort and exertion etched in the children's features, he gave a shiver and looked away guiltily.

Tollychook had screwed his face up so tightly that his eyes had disappeared and his bottom lip was touching the underside of his nose, which he had bandaged with a handkerchief.

Perhaps it was the pain of that mouse bite that enabled him to remember so vividly the rodent that had wriggled in his arms. Up until then he had always been an unremarkable, dull-witted boy, but suddenly his imagination bounded ahead and he knew how the poor animal had felt. He was no longer wrestling with it but had swapped places. Gripped in a werling's arms, he squirmed to get free. To run into the nearest hole and hide with his whiskers trembling was all he craved, and he let out a high shriek.

Master Gibble stared at him gleefully. "The token!" he cried. "Don't forget the token!"

Almost without realizing what he was doing, Tollychook raised the fur in his hand to his nose and inhaled sharply.

With that—he wergled.

High into the air Tollychook jumped, jiggling and quivering as the forces within him were unleashed at last.

Immediately, he began to change. Before he landed back on the platform, a lustrous coat of fur sprouted all over his skin. His breeches flew off as a pink tail whisked into existence behind him, and his jerkin was sent flying into the branches overhead when he thrashed his dwindling arms.

Down he tumbled, wearing only his snookulhood and the handkerchief still wrapped about his whiskery nose.

Onto the platform he fell, springing back up again and squeaking in amazement when he stared at the paws that had replaced his hands.

Master Gibble snorted diffidently. The transformation was not the greatest success he had overseen. The mouse that was now trying to control the movements of its tail was still recognizably Tollychook. It had the same nose and mouth, and the ears were not quite right.

"Adequate for a first attempt," the tutor commented. "Let us hope it will improve with practice."

Tollychook was too busy hopping up and down, admiring his new form, to take any notice.

"Looky me!" he cried in a trembling, mouselike voice. "Looky me!"

But the other children were absorbed in their own exertions. Then there came a small shout as another was jolted into his new shape, and there were suddenly two mice standing upon the platform.

All at once the rest of the youngsters gave astonished cries, fistfuls of fur were sniffed, and pink tails came sweeping from their clothes.

His eyes clamped shut, Gamaliel Tumpin heard the marvelous transformations erupt around him, and his anxiety mounted. Every new mouse gave a triumphant squeak as it bounced into being, and he began to panic. He didn't want to be left behind, but his fears upset his concentration and the memories of the hunt faded from his mind.

Gritting his teeth, he summoned them back, only to lose them again when the unmistakable voices of Mufus and Bufus proclaimed that they, too, had wergled successfully.

Blindly, he wondered how many others remained unchanged, like himself. Excited squeaks seemed to come from all directions, and he huffed and strained, exerting every ounce of strength.

"Come on, Gamaliel." Kernella's impatient call came ringing in his ears. "Hurry up!"

Her brother was frantic. Why couldn't he do it? Desperately he struggled to imagine he was a mouse.

"Please, please, please!" he begged, his voice cracking with effort and emotion.

Finally, the last of the other children wergled, and Gamaliel stood alone in a crowd of half-dressed and jubilant mice.

Flustered and close to tears, he made one last, despairing attempt.

Clutching the tuft of white fur to his nose, he took an enormous breath and doubled over, groaning with the stress and strain. Gamaliel's head thumped and his eyes ached behind the scrunched-up lids. He felt his knees begin to shake and a curious buzzing filled his mind.

This was it, he thought, the wergling was beginning, and his heart soared.

Rejoicing, he leaped up, waiting for the tail to burst out behind.

Yet the miracle never happened. Instead of turning into a rodent, Gamaliel Tumpin swayed dizzily and staggered backward.

"Did it work...?" he mumbled with a slur. "Am...am I a mouse?"

A prickling darkness engulfed him, and Gamaliel went crashing to the floor. He had fainted.

# CHAPTER 5
# The Trooping Ride

It was dark when Finnen Lufkin ascended the mighty oak in which the Tumpin family lived. Cold starlight streaked through the branches above, and the waxing moon cast black veins of shadow across his upturned face.

Climbing effortlessly, Finnen heard the indistinct voices of the Dritch family as he passed the region where they had their dwelling and moved ever upward. The opening that led to old Mistress Woonak's residence was dark and silent, for she often retired early, but overhead, he could see the faint glow of a lantern spilling out along the branches. A solitary, plump figure was sitting there, dangling its legs and humming softly.

"Gamaliel?" Finnen called. "Is that you?"

The figure started, and the lantern was lowered so that its gentle light fell full on Finnen's face.

"Hello, Finnen!" a voice greeted in pleased surprise. "What you doin' here at this late hour?"

The boy clambered a little higher until the perch was reached and he sat next to the bearer of the lamp.

"Evenin', Kernella," he said. "I came to see how your brother was doing."

Kernella Tumpin twirled a finger in her lank hair and dismissed any talk of Gamaliel with a terse "Pfft!"

"Is he feeling any better?" Finnen persisted.

The girl yawned. "Don't care," she replied. "Them Doolans is right: He is a useless lump. Ain't no one never swooned werglin' into a mouse before. Did you hear how that Stookie Maffin giggled with her friends?"

"Is he inside?" Finnen interrupted.

Kernella's brows twitched with irritation. "Don't you want to know what that sparrow-legged gnat-brain said to me?" she asked indignantly.

"No," came his blunt answer as he rose and stepped back along the branch. "Look, if Gamaliel is indoors, I'll go find him."

Kernella waited until Finnen was just about to step into the small passage leading to the Tumpin home, then she coughed.

"He ain't in there," she said. "Besides, if you go in now you'll be sorry. Father's in one of his story moods, and he'll bore the ears off you if you let him. Why do you think I'm out here?"

"So where is Gamaliel?" Finnen asked.

Kernella pointed upward. "In his favorite spot," she said. "Likes to go an' watch the world from up there—'specially when he's done something gormless or he's downright glum. Seems to me as how that's most of the time."

Not waiting to listen, Finnen hurried up the oak's uppermost boughs to where the branches divided, tapering into long, elegant fingers that brushed and scoured the night.

There, sitting upon the last twigs strong enough to support him, was Gamaliel Tumpin. This was his special, private place. Kernella was too heavy to pester him here, and from this vantage point he could gaze out across the forest roof and lose himself in dreams.

With the cool night breeze playing over his face, Gamaliel stared into the blank darkness of Hagwood and found it comforting. No one there knew how worthless he was, and he wished he had the courage to run away—into the heart of the forest.

"Best to be devoured by a wolf than stay here with everyone laughin' at me," he said sorrowfully. "An' better to get it over with quick. If I sit here long enough, maybe that owl Mr. Mattock talked about will swoop down and cart me off."

"You going to sit there feeling sorry for yourself all night?" Finnen asked suddenly.

Gamaliel turned, and the twigs swayed beneath him. "Leave me alone," he pleaded.

"If you really want me to, I will."

"I do. I don't want none of your pity."

Finnen shrugged. "I wasn't going to offer any," he said, preparing to return down the oak. "Only came to see if you fancied joining me on an excursion tonight. Doesn't matter. I can easily go on my own."

The older boy shinned down the branch, but Gamaliel called him back.

"Wait!" he cried. "Where you off to?"

Finnen chuckled. "Only way to find out is to come with me," he said mysteriously.

Gamaliel considered for a moment, then scrambled from the bobbing twigs and followed Finnen down.

The route Finnen took as he descended avoided the branch where Kernella sat in waiting. Instead, he climbed down the far side of the tree and hoped that she had not seen them.

Quickly they moved, as silently and as swiftly as werlings can. Then, into the soft leaf mold piled over the tree's roots, Finnen dropped—followed by Gamaliel.

"It's not safe to traipse through the wood at night," Gamaliel said, gazing apprehensively around at the moon-glimmering darkness. "It looks so different; I don't know if I dare."

Finnen began walking down the slope. "You'll be perfectly safe with me to guide you," he promised. "I prefer the wood at night. I've roamed in the dark hundreds of times before."

"If you're sure," Gamaliel said, scampering after him. "We going to see that old mouse again?"

Before Finnen could answer there came a "thud" in the

leaves behind, and there was Kernella—arms folded and annoyed.

"Don't you try and slip off without me," she said crossly. "If you don't let me join you, I'll tell."

There was nothing Finnen could do but allow her to accompany them, and so the three werlings set off into the midnight wood.

Under the towering black columns of the trees they journeyed, traveling northward, quite the opposite direction to the one Gamaliel had supposed. He had never been on the ground after dark, and the unfamiliar sights, smells, and sounds alarmed and thrilled him. He could not guess where Finnen was taking them, and he did not care. To be out wandering in the rich gloom was enough.

Kernella had already forgiven Finnen for trying to leave her behind. She had seen the wood wearing its nighttime raiment before and was glad simply to be plodding alongside her hero.

Listening politely to her chatter, Finnen Lufkin led them along forgotten pathways, over the gleaming ribbons of foraging snails, through dells thronging with rising toadstools, and into tunnels of dead fern.

Enchanted, Gamaliel said nothing. At length the trees began to thin on their left, and he caught a glimpse of the cinder track beyond.

Catching his breath, he stared fearfully through the outlying oaks. That neglected trail marked the edge of his world, and to be this close to it caused the hairs on his ears to tingle.

There was no time to stand and gape, however, for

Finnen and Kernella had tramped on, and Gamaliel saw only a brief vision of the barren heath in the distance, dim and gray under the moon.

Scuttling after the others, he heard his sister asking Finnen once more where they were headed.

"It isn't far now," came the cryptic answer as Finnen veered to the right.

The cinder track was left behind, and Gamaliel gradually began to hear the sounds of flowing water filtering through the trees ahead. They were drawing near to the Hagburn.

"Oh, Finnen!" Kernella chided when she realized where they were bound. "It's not allowed to jump the stream and go into the big forest. You know that."

Finnen chortled. "Don't worry," he said. "This is as close as we get to the Hagburn. Past those birches yonder and we'll be done."

Rearing like pillars of marble, glowing faintly in the moonlight, a row of birch trees formed a long colonnade through the wood. Both Kernella and Gamaliel were eager to see what lay behind.

Running the remaining distance, they scampered between the coldly glimmering trunks and stared about them.

Kernella pulled a disappointed face. The woodland looked no different in front of the birches, nothing special here at all—except for a grassy path that wound deep into the forest.

Her brother was not so easily discouraged. Close by, a large boulder jutted from the ground, and curious, Gamaliel pattered over to inspect it.

The rock was many times his height. Entering the deep lake of its shadow, Gamaliel ran his fingers over the lichen-speckled granite. Up to the sky the black shape jabbed, like the tip of an enormous sword threatening the starry heavens.

"It's called the Hag's Finger," Finnen informed him. "A Dooit Stone. It marks the northernmost boundary of werling land."

"There's scratches gouged into it down here," Gamaliel chirped suddenly. "Must have been there ever so long, fair near wore away they are now."

"Dooit writing," Finnen said. "It were the Dooits who put the Hag's Finger here many, many years ago."

"Who were they?" Gamaliel asked.

Brushing his long fringe from his face, Finnen leaned against the tall rock. "The Dooits were big folk who lived clear over the other side of Hagwood, nigh to a thicket of yew. Very wise they were, but cruel with it. Old tales tell of how they loved to slit throats on stones like these."

Gamaliel withdrew his hand quickly as though the granite had bitten him. Finnen laughed and shook his head.

"I'm sure they didn't do that here," he said, giving the Dooit Stone a friendly slap. "In them far-off yews there's supposed to be a great table of rock, and that was where the Dooits did all the killin'."

Behind them, Kernella stamped her feet and looked bored. "You mean to say we've come all this way to look at a giant pebble?" she demanded.

"No," Finnen replied, grinning as he slid his back down the rock and sat upon the grass. "This is only where we're going to wait. You'll see a lot more—I swear it."

The indifference vanished from Kernella's face, and she hurried to plump herself down by Finnen's side.

"What will we see?" she cried. "What? What?"

"Hush!" the boy told her. "From now on we must talk only in whispers."

Casting a critical eye at the moon, he nodded, then murmured, "Not much longer to go."

"What for?" Gamaliel asked, almost as impatiently as his sister.

Finnen looked at them both. "Don't you know what night this is?" he asked, slightly shocked.

"The night we get warmed leftovers," Kernella said with a grimace. "It'll be crusty nut pie tomorrow, though."

The boy sighed wearily. "During the year," he began, "there are certain times that are...special—when strange things happen. You must have heard tell of the folk who live in the great green hill."

"The lords and ladies!" Gamaliel cried, forgetting to whisper. "The royal court of the High Lady. I done heard all the stories our dad knows. I loves to hear about them, with their jewels and crowns and magic."

Finnen smiled. "Well, it's obvious that your father didn't tell you one story," he said, "or you'd realize why we're here. The one about the Trooping Ride—those four nights of the year when the Hollow Hill opens up and the Unseelie Court is compelled to ride forth."

Gamaliel stared at him in disbelief. "No!" he uttered in a voice trembling with excitement.

"This very night is one of those four," Finnen affirmed, his grin widening every instant. "From the hill the High Lady and her nobles range through Hagwood, parading along her borders and passing this very spot! I've always meant to come and see but never have."

A gurgle of bliss bubbled from Gamaliel's lips, and he threw himself backward, kicking his legs in the air.

Sitting beside Finnen, Kernella was still doubtful. "How'd you know all this?" she asked. "I never heard no one mention it afore. If'n it's true, why ain't there more come here to gawk?"

"My old nan knows more history than what's set down in Master Gibble's books of lore," Finnen answered. "It was she who told me about the Dooits, and many more things beside. You ever want to hear a real cracking yarn, you go ask her."

Kernella still was not convinced, but Finnen had leaned forward and was peering along the avenue of birches.

"Quick!" he hissed excitedly. "Make sure you're well hidden behind the rock. Can you see—over there?"

The Tumpin children looked to where his quivering fingers were pointing, and Gamaliel clapped his hand over his mouth to stop himself yelling for joy.

In the distance, through the trees, many lights were flickering. The lamps of the Hollow Hill had green flames, and because the bearers were still too far away to see, it seemed as if they were floating upon the shadow-filled air. Like a wavering procession of emerald stars, the lights moved through the wood, gradually approaching the rock that Finnen and the others were hiding behind.

Gamaliel heard the sound of hooves thudding the turf and began to see glimpses of indistinct figures revealed in the lamplight.

Up the grassy way the court of the Hollow Hill came, and the werlings were struck with awe and fear. Against the Hag's Finger they crouched, not wishing to be seen, yet

71

aching to see all. Kernella pulled the neck of her snookul-hood over her nose and covered her arms and legs with her cape, while Finnen took shallow breaths and became as still as the stone that concealed him. Soon the light of the lanterns filled their eyes, and the woodland was awash with the radiance of the underground realm.

The figures were so tall and menacing that Gamaliel wanted to shriek and run away. He had never seen any creature so large. He could not comprehend how they managed to walk without falling over. Yet in spite of his fears, he remained where he was, terrified and enchanted.

At the forefront of the faerie host marched a band of pages. These were kluries, squat creatures with broad, flat heads and tiny darting eyes that gleamed beneath low brows. Their arms reached down to the ground, and they were dressed in bloodred velvet with golden buttons. In their large hands they bore slender poles from which silver lanterns hung. The green fires within blazed fiercely.

The werlings shrank further into the fleeting shadows. The eyes of the pages were horribly vigilant, but swinging the lamps before them, they moved on into the forest, and the next group of creatures paraded into view.

Here were the esquires, blue-faced bogles every one. Their features were pinched and leering, and their pallid skins ashen gray in the glow of the lanterns, which were fashioned into the crests of their bronze helms. They were taller than the pages and wore leather hauberks painted with the emblem of the High Lady: a black owl wearing a golden crown. Their hauberks were so long that only their feet could be seen beneath, and over their shoulders they bore cruel-looking spears with jagged blades. Three ranks deep they trooped by, but there were so many of them that Gamaliel lost count at forty-seven.

Then came the goblin knights. Mounted upon horses bred beneath the ground, they were ghastly to behold. Their bodies were round and stocky, and they were clad in armor that shimmered like rippling water. They were fearsome beings of the chill earth. The grim features that poked from beneath their plumed helmets were covered in gray scales, and their eyes were dark hollows in which no glint of reflected light could be seen. Lances tipped with gold were carried in their clawed hands, and round shields bearing the owl badge were lashed across their shoulders. It was their coal black steeds that Gamaliel feared most of all.

They, too, were bedecked in armor and appeared more mechanical than living beasts. Their eyes burned with scarlet fire, and blasts of steam erupted from their nostrils like the furious shriek of some internal engine. The forest floor was pounded by their silver-shod hooves, and as they paraded past, a ray of red shone full onto Gamaliel's face.

Horrified, he ducked, expecting the nightmare to thunder over him and smash his bones into the soil. But nothing happened, and when he next dared to raise his head, he saw that the knights had gone and a new regiment of fearsome folk was passing the Dooit Stone.

There marched the Redcaps, the High Lady's hideous foot soldiers. Lolling upon hunched shoulders, their large, unwieldy heads were foul and grotesque. Over their bald, bony skulls they wore tight-fitting hats that were steeped in blood, and the crimson juice had dribbled down their foul faces, staining their piglike snouts.

Gamaliel eyed those snuffling noses uneasily. The Red-caps had caught a scent that was unfamiliar to them and were gibbering to themselves in puzzlement. It was the wer-lings they could smell, but thankfully none of them thought to probe the shade beneath the standing stone, and they shuffled morosely on.

The thump of hoof-falls heralded the advance of more horses, yet these were not the sable war beasts favored by the goblin knights. The steeds that followed the Redcaps were as gray as a rain-soaked dawn, and upon their backs rode the nobles of the Hollow Hill.

At the first glimpse, Gamaliel forgot the fear that the preceding folk had instilled in him. The lords and ladies of the court were the fairest creatures he had ever seen.

They were sumptuously arrayed in silks edged with gold and silver brocade. Velvet cloaks trimmed with lustrous fur were clasped about their necks by brooches set with gems that sparkled and flashed in the lamplight.

Staring fixedly before them, they held their heads high. Every face was proud and haughty, but they owned an ethe-real beauty that made Kernella curdle inside, and she pouted when she saw the enamored expression that had stolen over Finnen.

With a swish of the last horse's tail, the nobles rode ahead, and trampling behind came the royal bodyguard.

After the splendor and grace of the nobles, the spectacle of the guards was like waking from a sweet dream and dis-covering that you have been sleeping in a dung heap.

They were spriggans, fierce fighters clad from head to toe in clinking mail. Pale and yellow were the slits of their eyes, and every warty jaw was crammed with needle-sharp fangs. Swords twice the length of themselves were carried upon their backs, and knotted whips were tucked into their belts, together with a deadly assortment of knives and curved daggers. Great was their number, and the din of their passing was brutal and harsh. Yet in their midst, riding a silver-white mare, was the most stunning vision of all.

"There," Finnen murmured in a hallowed whisper. "That must be her, the High Lady herself—Rhiannon of the Green Hill."

Even Kernella gasped with amazement, and Gamaliel felt as though he wanted to cry.

Beneath a silken canopy embroidered with jewels and golden thread, held up by four of her repugnant bodyguards, rode a woman whose beauty outshone the lanterns. Lovely as a winter night was she; her raven hair was like a trailing cloud of storm, and a circlet of gold sat lightly upon her pale brow. Cold majesty radiated from her divine face, and the unearthly light of the hidden realm bloomed in her cheeks. Her eyes were dark and keen, and they pierced the surrounding gloom, laying all secrets bare. Yet they were not turned to the Dooit Stone, and Gamaliel almost sprang out of hiding to draw her attention. It would probably be the last thing that he ever did, but at least his death would be filled with the sight of her looking at him.

The impulse faded and he was glad, for there was a hardness about those fine, delicate features. They almost looked as if they had been hammered from crystal.

On she rode, dressed in a gown of rippling twilight, with a hooded cloak made entirely from owl feathers hanging from her shoulders. She was a living, breathing enchantment.

When she drew level with the Hag's Finger, the werlings

saw for the first time that upon the lap of the Lady Rhiannon was a small figure. Gamaliel had not seen its like before. The lurid light of the lanterns could not diminish the ruddy warmth of its chubby flesh, and the High Lady held it close, within a fold of her feathered mantle.

"What is it?" Gamaliel breathed.

Finnen waited until horse and rider had passed. Then, with an eye upon the straggling spriggans, he whispered. "That was a mortal infant. He was taken to the Hollow Hill many years ago. If he were ever to return to his own kind then old age would claim him and death would follow."

Into the forest the cavalcade journeyed, and the woodland behind was plunged back into darkness as the last of the lamps was carried into the far distance.

Stepping from the shelter of the standing stone, Finnen Lufkin crept out onto the woodland path. There was no indication that the Unseelie Court had gone by: Not a blade of grass was broken, and the soil showed no sign of hoof marks.

Standing there, Finnen watched until the strings of emerald lights bobbed behind the furthest trees and disappeared completely.

"Glory!" Gamaliel exclaimed. "Shall we follow them and see where they go?"

Finnen shook his head and restrained him, for Gamaliel was already padding after them.

"We wouldn't be welcome," he told him. "Deep into the heart of Hagwood they're headed, and will hold high revel when they get there. They won't allow outsiders to spy on them, certainly not a trio of werlings. We're nothing to them, beneath their consideration, but they'd skewer us on spikes if they caught us tagging along uninvited."

Gamaliel stared into the night-shrouded forest, then turned to his new friend. "Thank you for showing me this," he said. "Not being able to wergle into a mouse don't seem half as important anymore."

"Good!" Finnen declared. "There really is no reason to panic next time you try. You'll do it; just be patient."

Combing her fingers through her hair, Kernella threw Finnen a furtive glance then said, "You know, that Lady would have been a lot prettier if'n her hair had been red— don't you think so?"

Finnen suppressed a chuckle. "It's definitely time we headed back" was his only comment.

Returning through the birches, the three werlings retraced their steps. Gamaliel felt a lot happier, and delighted in picking up odds and ends from the woodland floor. Into his wergle pouch he popped them: wispy tufts of hares' tails, stray feathers, and another pebble to add to his collection. Finding a long twig, he held it over his shoulder, remembering how the goblin knights had carried their gold-tipped lances, then went cantering ahead, snorting down his nose like their fearsome steeds.

Walking beside Finnen, Kernella watched her brother disapprovingly. "I don't know why you bother with him," she said.

Finnen fingered his own wergle pouch, which he hardly needed to use anymore.

"When I was his age I was more nervous and hopeless than Gamaliel," he told her. "I wish that there had been someone to help me then, someone to steer me on the right track and encourage me. Things might have worked out a lot differently."

He sighed dismally, and Kernella scratched her head in confusion.

"But you're the best at everything!" she cried. "Better than all the rest of us—you'll even show up old Gibble one of these days."

The hero of the werling children avoided her eyes. Kernella did not understand; how could she? No one would ever know unless he confessed. Finnen chewed his bottom lip in silence as he brooded on the awful crime he had committed. His secret was far too shameful to tell to anyone.

# CHAPTER 6
# The Wandering Smith

Even as the three young werlings returned to their homes, beyond the eaves of Hagwood a lone figure slowly labored along the cinder track.

From the far north he had journeyed, but no one place was his home, no roots did his feet put down, and for more years than he dared remember the lands had rolled ceaselessly beneath him. Too long he had roamed where he willed. He was a creature of the earth, a Pucca, but he had forsworn the delved halls of his birth, choosing against nature to live in the world of mortal men. There, he was deemed a midget, a stunted curiosity to be taunted and laughed at, but all their scorn and ridicule seemed better to him than the darkness he had left behind.

Down the years the oddness of his appearance had served him well, keeping unwanted interest at bay. An iron helm was always jammed firmly upon his head, and his hair was long and unkempt. A thick, wiry brown beard reached down to his waist, and his face was habitually coated in grime. An apron of hide, blackened and singed from the forge, flapped across his knees, and bands of hammered metal covered his wrists. About his neck he wore innumerable charms and amulets, and although they were hidden beneath his beard, they made their presence known by clacking and clattering together when he walked.

In the towns and villages he visited, the Pucca was a recognizable, albeit rare, figure. He told his true name to no one, thus they christened him by his trade and his nomadic existence—he was the Wandering Smith.

Yet now he was weary. His beard was flecked with gray, and his back was bent by the relentless measures of time and the burden that he had borne. It had been a difficult and grave decision to make, but finally he had resolved to return to the land of his past and confront the torments that plagued his conscience. The wrongs of yore should be punished, and he was the only one who could accomplish that.

With his head bowed he trod the overgrown path, pulling the covered handcart that contained his tools and scant belongings behind him. The crunching of the wheels over the stones and cinders was the only sound to be heard, and the Pucca's face became grim. The surrounding silence was unnatural, and the cart began to bounce even more noisily as he hastened on his way.

"A few furlongs more," he muttered uneasily. "If the Smith recalls aright, Moonfire Farm lies at the end of this forsaken road. Unless the evil has grown strong enough to leave the forest, Smith should be able to bed down in the barn this night. When he's settled in the straw and had a chance to think, then he'll know what's best. Mornin's the right time for what he's got to do; no use in this dead dark—perilous maybe."

The bright green eyes of his kind shone in the murk as he looked warily around. The landscape had altered little in the spinning years, but he tried to push the returning memories to a far corner of his mind.

"Good hot supper, that's what the Smith is wanting," he said, trying to turn his thoughts aside. "If there's a light showing in the farmhouse, he'll sharpen the mistress's knives and shoe the master's horse in fair barter. A mutton stew would go down real easy. Ah, he'd like that now, would old Smith."

The Pucca spurred himself on, but after only a few short minutes, the wheels of the handcart rattled to a stop, and the Wandering Smith murmured unhappily.

He'd cornered a bend in the track, and the concealing trees upon his left now disclosed a long stretch of the neglected road ahead. In the near distance the Pucca saw a sinister framework looming over the wayside.

It was a gibbet, an old forgotten gallows. In former times,

highwaymen would be strung up there as a gruesome warning to the other gentlemen of the road. Silhouetted in the moonlight, the timbers looked stark and threatening. But it was not the gibbet that had caused the Smith to halt and anxiously clutch at the talismans about his neck.

Perched upon the projecting arm was a large barn owl. In the darkness its eyes burned like molten gold, and their unblinking stare was fixed upon the Pucca.

"By the dragon's sulfurous breath!" the Smith swore. "That's no ordinary bird."

Turning cautiously, he wondered if he ought to go back. But he knew that only the empty wild stretched behind him. There would be no hope of shelter or protection out there. His one chance was to press on and gain, if he could, the safety of the farm.

Grasping the handles of the cart once more, he prepared to make a dash for it. Yet before he could take flight, the owl shook its feathers and opened its beak. From that lofty height a cold, condemning voice rang out across the track, and the Smith trembled to hear it.

"Witless thief!" it called. "Witless thief! Didst thou truly believe thy vagabonding would go unmarked? Thou cannot set thy accursed feet within my Lady's realm and elude the vigilance of those in Her service."

The Pucca steadied himself and glared at the bird. "Since when did the lands beyond the fringes of Dunrake fall under Her dominion?" he cried. "Has the heartless one grown so great?"

A hideous cackle sounded from the downy throat, and the owl's fierce eyes opened wider still.

"Yea, indeed," it crowed. "My Lady has thriven in the years of thy absence. Far now does Her power reach, and never more shalt thou escape Her."

His face twisted with disdain, the Smith spat upon the ground, and the owl screeched in rage.

"Petty cur!" it shrieked. "Base despoiler! Surrender unto me that which thou stole and thy death shall be swift."

Beneath the Pucca's dark brows there flickered a glint of green, and he reached into his cart.

"Smith knows what you're needing," he said. "And fain he'll be to deliver it."

Suddenly he whirled about, and in his hands he wielded a loaded crossbow.

"Here's an end to your service, Master Flat Face!" he yelled, taking careful aim. "May all felons be so dispatched!"

But before the bolt could fly into the owl's breast, the bird laughed.

"Long years has my mistress spent preparing the welcome of thy return," it scorned, devoid of fear. "Now, indeed, thou shalt pay for thy malfeasance."

And with that, it spread its wings and let loose a loud, summoning call.

At once a chilling, bloodthirsty yell answered, and the Smith faltered.

Other cries went shrieking into the night, and the Pucca stared wildly about him as the trap was sprung.

The shadowy dark upon the right-hand side of the track suddenly seethed with frenzied movement and evil voices. Countless pale eyes snapped open and twisted shapes leaped up from the stubbly grass. Out of the gloom they sprang, and the Smith quailed when at last he beheld them—the thorn ogres.

As tortured shrubs of briar and bramble they appeared. Tangled branches, covered in cruel barbs and spikes, thrust from their backs and crowned their heads. Their faces were masks of brimming hatred, and every deformed feature was molded and ruined by malevolence.

Onto the track they charged, the stumped ends of their bowed, buckled legs thumping and dragging over the ground. In the remote cold hills they had been bred to slaughter and destroy, and their mouths gaped wide with the lust for murder that had been nurtured in them. The ghastly light that welled in their bulging eyes was an unholy glare fueled by loathsome hungers. They lurched for their victim, hissing and cackling with boiling malice.

The first of the monstrous creatures to leap onto the track was as big as a calf: a huge, malignant brute with a thick, woody tail that creaked and groaned as it lashed from side to side. A wintry hedge of spines reared over its hump back, and from its grinning maw a grotesque, hollow voice came growling.

"Bite and tear," it rumbled menacingly. "Rip and spike."

"Seize the traitorous thief!" the owl commanded. "In thy mistress's name, take and bind him!"

The Smith was too stricken and daunted to move. Vital moments were wasted as the horror rushed toward him. Three more swift, hobbling strides and the fiend's outstretched claws would clutch and clench at him—and the struggle would be over before it had commenced.

Yet in the Pucca's chest his courage kindled urgently.

Snarling, he swung the crossbow about and the bolt went singing into the night.

Deep inside the ogre's throat the dart plunged, and a startled shriek bellowed from the punctured gullet.

Like a hewn tree, the nightmare toppled to the ground. Thrashing the tail, it choked its last breath, but there were many others to replace it.

Over the fallen leader three more instantly came bounding, and there was no time to reload the crossbow.

"Witch's filth!" the Smith cried, hurling the weapon at their vile faces and unfastening the sheath of the small knife that hung at his belt.

But the ogres were too fast. Before he could even grasp the hilt, their claws were upon him.

Yammering in barbaric, callous voices, they flung him to the ground, the thorny talons scratching and pinching his flesh as they pinned him down. Strong and immovable as the roots of ancient trees was their fearsome grip, and there was nothing the Smith could do. He was caught.

Lying across the track, his eyes turned to the star-filled heavens, he saw the abominations gather around him. There were ten of them, and all were croaking wickedly, promising death and torment.

"Strangle and gouge!" they taunted. "Sip blood—be strong."

From somewhere outside the range of the Pucca's sight a higher, squeaking voice cried, "He killed Ungark—stick him! Gore him!"

The Smith tried to turn his head, but the claws gripped him too fiercely. It was only when the owner of that voice came pushing through the crowded ogres to lean directly over his face that he saw there was an eleventh member of that foul crew.

It was a mean, ratlike specimen, much smaller than the rest. Upon its head the twigs sprouted ragged leaves, and its eyes were narrow and sly.

"Much juice in him," it declared, squeezing the Pucca's cheeks and slavering eagerly. "Snaggart want—Snaggart bite—Snaggart empty!"

The ogre smacked its unclean lips and licked its fangs, but high above the track there came a forbidding cry, and the owl came swooping from the gibbet.

"Stem thine appetite," the bird commanded, dropping from the night with its wings spread wide. "Not yet shalt thou dine."

The small ogre slapped its sharp nose and waggled its ears in fury, but the owl dived down behind and, with a flick of its talons, sent the creature stumbling backward.

There was a rush of white feathers and the bird alighted upon the Smith's chest.

"No, not yet," the owl said, its golden eyes staring at the Pucca's upturned face. "Not till the thief yields that most precious thing that he stole."

A defiant chuckle came from the Smith's lips, and the owl juddered upon his chest.

"Insolent dolt!" the bird snapped. "Quickly shall we tame thy want of manners. Give unto me that which thou took those many years ago. Such is the demand of my Lady and thou cannot deny Her. Return it without delay!"

A bleak smile broadened in the grizzled beard. "Do you really believe the Smith has it?" he laughed. "Oh no, Master

Flat Face. He assures you he does not. If that thing were, indeed, in his possession, do you think he would have balked to do what must be done? Nay, your mistress would have perished ages since if it were his. Again he says, he does not have that which you seek."

The owl dug its talons into the Pucca's chest, piercing the thick hide of the apron and pricking the layers of clothing beneath.

"Yet thou knowest where this treasure is bestowed," it said with menace. "When thou fled the Hollow Hill, whither did thou run? In what place did thy light fingers conceal it?"

The Smith made no reply, and the owl tugged viciously at his beard.

"Rigid tongues are easily loosened," the bird vowed. "Think not that thy neck is stiff enough to withstand the skill of our torture masters. They excel at their craft and love it most dearly."

"Your threats are idle," the Pucca scoffed. "She would not risk Smith's return to Her hill, not even to bear him to the deep places of the earth. Loud would be his accusing cries; he would make the very vaults ring with the condemning truth, and the entire court would know. Has She bribed and corrupted them all? Smith thinks not."

It was the owl's turn to laugh. "Simple fool," it mocked. "Did I not tell thee Her realm has grown great? Not to the royal halls wilt thou be borne, but to the cold hills beyond the Lonely Mere, where Her dungeons are deeper and none shall hear thee, though thou scream and howl in thine agonies. Verily thou shalt speak thy secret, the device shall be returned unto its true owner. Yet of thee...thou shalt wish there were more secrets to be spilled. Ignoble and wretched shall be thy deserved end."

Pleased with itself, the bird fluffed out its plumage and took to the air once more.

"Bear him up!" it ordered the thorn ogres. "Take his perfidious carcass over the heath and to the cold hills. Let the skilled attention of the torture masters pare the knowledge from him."

Into the night the owl soared, and the monsters that held the Smith hoisted him off the ground.

Beneath him the smallest ogre darted, the leafy spike of its head poking him maliciously in the back.

"Snaggart jump," it barked. "Snaggart give pain."

A dreary chant came from the others as they lifted the Pucca over their heads and marched toward the barren heath.

"Back to hills—return to caves," they sang.

Carried aloft in their iron grasp, the Smith was still unable to struggle or even move his limbs, but he was not conquered yet.

"Thimbleglaive!" he called abruptly. "Fly out! Fly out! Strike Smith's foes and cause a rout."

As soon as the words were spoken, the small knife at his belt flew from its sheath and magically shot into the air. For an instant the moonlight flashed across the spinning blade, then down it sped. Into the claws that held the Smith the keen edge went slicing, severing knobbled fingers and biting into gnarled wrists.

Yowls of pain erupted on all sides as the enchanted knife thrust and jabbed, weaving a net of cold and deadly light about its master. Roaring, the thorn ogres dropped their captive and fell back, flailing their gashed and mutilated arms. Black blood splashed onto the cinders, and their branches clattered and shook as they stamped and screamed.

Circling above them, the owl cried out in rage. "Stand firm!" it screeched. "What is the bite of a single blade? Hold him! Seize him!"

But the ogres were dismayed and staggered back. There were not enough of them to withstand the unexpected onslaught, and the ghastly light of their eyes was dimmed. Cutting through the shadows, the knife speared the slowest in the neck and the monster fell to the ground with a heavy thud.

In the confusion the Smith leaped to his feet. Behind him the smallest ogre groaned, for the Pucca's fall had crushed it to the floor and many of its twigs were snapped and broken.

"Pounce upon him!" the owl demanded, beating its wings before the ogres' hideous faces. "Do not let him go free!"

Yet they were too cowed and afraid to obey. The knife was a frightful opponent, and they hissed in revolt.

Snatching his chance, the Smith ran to his cart and called. "Home, Thimbleglaive. Home!"

Rushing through the air, the knife switched direction and flew at once back into its sheath.

A roguish grin lit the Pucca's grimy face as he turned to the infuriated owl and snapped his fingers at it.

"Tell the tyrant Her doom is at hand," he cried. Then, dragging the cart behind him, he darted through the trees upon his left and plunged into the dark eaves of Hagwood.

Incensed, the owl squawked a string of oaths and curses

after him before returning its wrathful attention to the thorn ogres.

"Craven beasts!" it shrieked. "Thy deaths are no matter. Supreme is thy failure: The traitor has gone. She will know of it. She will punish thee."

Nursing their wounds, the ogres shuddered and hid their faces. Picking itself from the floor, Snaggart glared into the wood and scampered toward the outlying trees.

"We fetch!" it yapped. "Snaggart hurt—Snaggart sting."

The others lumbered behind it, but the owl flew before them.

"Ye cannot enter the forest this night!" it forbade them. "The Unseelie Court is abroad, and your presence would be detected. Should the hillmen capture you, then all Her plots and designs would go amiss. The hour has not come for the denizens of the Hollow Hill to know of your existence. The two secrets are bound together."

The ogres muttered in their empty voices, and Snaggart leaped up and down.

"Thief! Thief!" it jabbered. "Snaggart find—Snaggart kill!"

"Obey me!" the owl demanded. "The traitor is now beyond thy reach. Get thee to the heath and there await the rest of thy kind. Thy number must be many times the greater before Hagwood may be invaded."

Snaggart jerked its head forward and peered into the shadows that lay beneath the trees, its squinting eyes swiveling from side to side.

"Snaggart not like," it grumbled. "Want kill—drink blood."

The barn owl glowered at it, and the small ogre shrank away. "All of you begone!" the bird declared. "There will be feasting aplenty before our work is ended. Till ye are summoned again, stay upon the scrubland. The arch felon shall not evade us. Within the forest there are many eyes in the employ of our mistress. Let the thief believe he has escaped, then surely he will lead us straight to the very thing we seek."

Woeful and mumbling, the thorn ogres retreated back over the cinder trackway and began lurching across the heath.

Gingerly touching the weeping stumps of its broken twigs, Snaggart watched the snowy shape of the barn owl rise above the trees, and a mutinous leer spread over the creature's grotesque features.

"Snaggart wait," it snarled. "But Snaggart empty."

# CHAPTER 7
# Games and Stories

Brilliant sunshine flooded through the trees that grew west of the Hagburn. The warm light of spring reached into every corner and danced in the reflected cheer of the primroses that had risen through the carpeting dead leaves.

That morning all spirits were high, and in the hazel tree the young werlings were treated to a wergling display by the older children.

Sitting upon the platform, even Gamaliel felt light of heart, and he watched in admiration as the transformations took place before him.

This was the time when the elder students proved how

hard they had practiced during the winter months. With their wergle pouches at the ready, they changed themselves into all manner of small woodland creatures. There were stoats, snails, squirrels and voles, rats, and several unsuccessful finches and sparrows.

Master Gibble eyed the dismal birds ruefully. They looked plucked and naked. "Feathers are extremely difficult to achieve," he said haughtily. "And your legs are hopeless—far too fat and bending in all the wrong places. If your ambition compels you to attempt forms that are beyond your capabilities, do not presume to parade the disastrous results before me."

When it was Kernella's turn, she took from her pouch a neatly bound bunch of fur and gave it a tremendous sniff while muttering her wergling word under her breath. At once her ears flapped and stretched upward. A fluffy tail popped out from under her cape, and her legs became twice their normal size. In a matter of moments she became a fat baby rabbit, an illusion spoilt only by the gingery hair that hung about the ears, the innumerable freckles that speckled its fur, and the wide gap between its front buck teeth.

"Well done," Finnen congratulated her.

The rabbit blushed with pride, but close by, Stookie Maffin gave a disparaging snort and immediately wergled into a shrew.

A honk of laughter came from Kernella's goofy mouth, and she promptly assumed her own form again.

"Hoo, Stookie!" she exclaimed. "How well you fit that there shape. What an honest-to-goodness shrew you are!"

Stookie squealed, and the wergled shape was discarded. "Better than being a fat dollopy rabbit!" she answered hotly.

Before the insults worsened, Master Gibble called for silence, then turned to Finnen Lufkin, who had, as yet, not changed into anything at all.

"And you, Master Lufkin," he said with forced cordiality. "Will you be joining your fellows, or is that beneath you nowadays?"

Finnen brushed the hair from his forehead, and a slow smile spread across his face. "I didn't know where to begin," he replied honestly.

"Are there, indeed, so many forms in your repertoire?" Master Gibble asked archly.

Finnen put his head to one side as he counted, then nodded. "Yes," he said, much to the tutor's consternation and annoyance. "There are."

A soft, whistling peep escaped from one of Master Gibble's nostrils, and he clenched his teeth together.

"Would you care to demonstrate?" he hissed. "If it isn't too much trouble. I'm sure we would all benefit enormously from such a display of your gift."

Ignoring the sarcasm, Finnen agreed, and removing the wergle pouch from his belt, let it fall to the floor. "Won't be needing that," he said.

Terser Gibble trembled with indignation, then held up his hand before the boy could begin. "A moment!" he cried. "As you are so proficient, why not make the performance a trifle more interesting for the others? I suggest that we both wergle together and see who falters first."

The children around them grew silent, and everyone resumed their normal shape. This had never happened before, and they looked at Finnen nervously. Would he accept the challenge?

"A friendly competition," Master Gibble goaded. "Nothing more."

Finnen was not certain, but he could see that the others were anxious for him to try. Kernella was staring at him expectantly, her eyebrows jiggling wildly up and down. The confidence they all had in him was overwhelming, and he knew there was no way out.

"Very well," he assented. "I'll do it."

The other werlings gave a glad cheer and ran to their seats, forming a clear stage where the contest could take place.

Swishing his gown around him, Master Gibble strode into the center, and Finnen followed.

"From the simplest through to the most sophisticated," the spindly tutor announced. "When you are ready, we shall begin."

Finnen took a deep breath and prepared himself. "Ready," he said.

Master Gibble struck a flamboyant pose, and his shape dissolved effortlessly down into the black creases of his gown.

A scrawny mouse with an inordinately long nose popped his head out of the collapsing robe and scurried free before the topmost fold fell.

Squeaking with vain pride, he turned, but saw that Finnen had already wergled and his mouse was staring back at him.

Master Gibble slapped his tail upon the deck. The face of Finnen's mouse was far more convincing than that of his own. With an irritated toss of the head, the tutor wergled into a hedgehog.

Yet Finnen did not accompany him, and Master Gibble wondered if the game already was won. Finnen had remained a mouse, but no—thrilled murmurs were fizzing through the audience, and when the tutor stared at his competitor he understood why.

With impertinent ease, Finnen was wergling into many different species. From a wood mouse he blended his shape into that of a dormouse, then he became a harvest mouse, and with a flick of his ears slipped into a gray house mouse.

The spines covering Master Gibble's hedgehog shape quivered, and the tutor transformed into a skinny rat. He ran at the mouse to cuff his head.

Too late he saw Finnen assume the hedgehog form and he drove his paws onto sharp bristles.

Squealing, the tutor shook himself, and his outline rippled as the remaining primitive forms were rapidly dispensed with in their correct order, from squirrel through to mole.

The speed of the changes was astonishing, and the watching children gasped with wonder, not daring to blink in case they missed the next new shape. Before them the figure of Master Gibble shifted endlessly; yet Finnen was not defeated. Shape for shape he matched the Great Grand Wergle Master until the list of simple forms was completed and the specialist section of the tournament commenced.

At once Master Gibble became a cream-colored ferret, but Finnen expertly eclipsed the move by wergling into a green-and-yellow frog. The ferret vanished and in its place was a newt, peppered with dark spots.

Finnen's frog leaped over the newt's head, but when he

landed he had become a lanky-legged rabbit, which hopped madly about the platform, taunting the newt with an impudent jig.

"That's it, Finnen!" the Doolan brothers called. "You're showing the old misery!"

The newt raised its head and glared at them imperiously, but Mufus and Bufus only snickered and mumbled behind their hands.

Gamaliel could not believe how splendidly Finnen was doing. His sister's infatuation and the other children's hero worship was more than explained.

Sitting in a corner by herself, Liffidia watched the competition intently. She wanted to shout out something rude and insulting to Master Gibble to put him off. But while she struggled for the appropriate heckling jibes, the newt moved and started to chase its tail. A moment later the glistening body had stretched in length, and there on the deck was an adder with a long tongue flicking between its oddly tapering jaws.

Liffidia forgot her insults, and the Doolans shuffled backward. Sitting beside Gamaliel, Tollychook began to fret, and Kernella's mouth dropped open.

Finnen's young hare was still oblivious to the new and deadly change that had occurred behind him. He continued to caper while the snake slithered close and reared its scaly head.

Frightened whimpers issued from the audience. For a dreadful instant they thought the adder would strike. At the crucial moment, however, the rabbit reached up with its front legs and two webs of leathery skin unfurled.

With a downward thrust of his new wings, the bat that Finnen had transformed into flitted up into the overhanging branches of the hazel. There, with the sunlight glowing redly through the fine membrane spanning his fingers, he acquired a perfect covering of feathers and perched upon one of the boughs as a wood lark.

"He can do feathers!" the children cried.

"And he can fly!" Kernella crowed, her devotion bursting out of its former bounds. "Ooh, Finnen—you never cracked on!"

Overhead, the wood lark opened its beak and, in a beautiful chirping voice, sang a piping cadence of notes as a finale. The werling children applauded enthusiastically and rose to their feet.

The snake's lidless eyes considered the sweetly singing bird for a moment, then the competition was over and the familiar, gangly figure of Master Gibble was standing there, wrapping his gown about him once more.

A somber expression was etched upon his face, and the tutor bowed so low to Finnen that his nose touched the floor and bent sideways.

"Your skill is, indeed, very great," he acknowledged. "In all these years of instruction, never have I had the privilege of teaching any pupil with such a gift as yours. This day I have seen my successor. You will be one of the grand adepts, Master Lufkin."

The wood lark hopped from its perch, and Finnen jumped onto the platform as himself. The children surged forward and clapped him on the back, praising his name and stamping so hard that the branches of the hazel tree quivered and shook. Finnen squirmed with discomfort under the gushing acclaim and wished he had never allowed himself to be persuaded into the foolish contest.

When the clamor and adulation subsided, Master Gibble returned to the serious matters of the day.

"Tonight you younger students will venture out into the wood and commence the next stage of instruction," he announced. "At sundown we shall reassemble here. Then, in the same groups as yesterday, you will remain outside all night and study the second animal on the wergling list. You all saw just now that it is the hedgehog. I want you to learn its ways and return at daybreak tomorrow with a token of prickly bristles to add to your wergle pouches—and remember to keep those pouches tidy!"

Hearing this, Gamaliel tucked his own velvety bag out of sight, for it still was stuffed with the gleanings of the woodland floor. The other werlings were extremely excited at the prospect of the nocturnal adventure, but those in Gamaliel's group knew that they were the luckiest of all—they were going to be led by Finnen.

THE rest of the day passed all too slowly for the impatient children. Most of them were put to bed in the afternoon so that they would not be too tired when darkness fell, but sleep eluded them all—except for Tollychook, who dropped off immediately.

Liffidia Nefyn was made to repeat the previous day's exercise. With Master Gibble standing over her, she caught a mouse and miserably plucked out a small amount of fur. Back at the hazel she was given another stern lecture on the do's and don'ts before she was finally permitted to wergle.

Liffidia did it beautifully, and impressed for the second time that day, the tutor was compelled to send her home to prepare for the next lesson.

Evening came at last. Streaks of scarlet striped the sky as the sun dipped behind the gathering clouds, and for a time Hagwood appeared aglow with angry flame.

Slowly the light faded, and the waiting shadows crept out under the trees. When the early stars winked above the forest, the children set off.

Into the woodland they trailed, splitting into their different groups and disappearing into the dark. The leaders each carried a lantern to illuminate the finer points of hedgehog behavior, and everyone was armed with a good strong stick in case of owl attack. It was going to be a long night, and bags of provisions were slung across the youngsters' shoulders.

For a brief while it looked as though Kernella wanted to join her party with that of Finnen's. But Master Gibble, who was keeping a watchful eye on the departures, shouted at her, and she scuttled away with her charges scampering after.

Gamaliel was relieved; he didn't want his sister bossing him about again.

Heading north, Finnen led them along much the same route as the previous night's journey to the Hag's Finger. But this time each of them would be forced to confront a terrible danger.

When the edge of the woodland was in sight and the heath dimly visible beyond, he called a halt, and by the roots of an ash tree they made their encampment.

"It's as likely a spot as any," he said, setting the lantern down. "Our prickly friends will be stirring soon, and they always come foraging between the wood and the heath."

Gamaliel and the others sat upon the ground, but Mufus Doolan stared out at the tantalizing expanse of the heath and whistled longingly.

"That looks better over there!" he argued. "Bet there's more hedgehogs in all that grass than you can find trundling through these leaves."

His brother agreed wholeheartedly. "I'm gonna go and see," he declared.

"Sit down!" Finnen told them. "No one's going over there. You're nowhere near ready to leave the shelter of the trees, and that wasteland is far too exposed. You'd be an owl's supper before you knew what had happened."

The Doolans kicked the leaves sullenly but joined the others in the circle they had formed around the lantern.

"How long will it be before we see a hedgehog?" Liffidia asked.

Finnen shrugged. "Could be hours yet," he answered.

The Doolans groaned and looked bored.

"What we gonna do till then?" Bufus complained.

Turning his gaze from one member of the company to another, his brother snickered at Tollychook, who was already tucking into the food from his bag. Mufus puffed out his cheeks and patted his stomach in mockery, but Tollychook was too engrossed in a delicious berry-and-chestnut pie to notice.

Mufus switched his attention to Gamaliel and nudged his brother. Young Master Tumpin was sorting through the treasures he had popped into his wergle pouch and was examining them carefully.

"Hoy, Gammy!" Mufus cried. "What's all that rubbish? Pointy-nosed Gibble would have a fit if he knew what you had in there! Just wait till I tell him!"

Gamaliel hurriedly refilled the pouch and looked worried.

Delighted to see that the threat had discomforted him, the Doolans decided to taunt some more.

"How you getting on with your wergling, Gammy?" they asked. "We've been practicing all afternoon. Real good at it, we are now."

Bringing out their tokens of fur, the brothers sniffed them and instantly changed into mice.

"Hardly takes any effort at all now!" they squeaked. "Shame you can't do it."

Gamaliel stared at the ground, but the Doolans kept wergling in and out of the mouse shapes and laughed at his forlorn expression.

"That's enough!" Finnen said crossly. "You'll exhaust yourselves doing that."

Reluctantly and with deliberate slowness, the Doolans returned to their normal forms.

"I could tell you a story if you like," Finnen suggested, hoping this bribe would prevent any more teasing. "I know lots of good ones from my nan."

Mufus and Bufus were not impressed, but Tollychook spluttered eagerly and sprayed crumbs of piecrust everywhere. "Yessy, please!" he said, the ends of the handkerchief that was still bound about his nose flapping madly.

"What about a tale of the hillfolk?" Gamaliel asked.

The Doolans muttered and curled their lips peevishly while Finnen searched his memory.

"No," Liffidia interrupted. "I'd like to know more about Frighty Aggie."

Finnen looked at her sharply. That particular tale was not one he would relish telling.

"I'm not sure I remember it properly," he mumbled.

"'Course you do!" the Doolans urged. "We like that one, we do."

Glancing round at the darkened wood, Finnen shivered. There were elements of the tale that touched too closely on his own secrets, but he could not deny the demands of his group now.

"All right," he began. "Frighty Aggie it is."

With the night close about them, the werlings huddled before the lantern, and the buttery light played over their faces as Finnen commenced the tragic history of the nightmare that haunted the dreams of infants.

"In long years past," the boy said, repeating the tale precisely as it had been told to him, "the instructor of the young was called Agnilla Hellekin...

"She was one of the great adepts of the werling folk, one of the finest champions of the art that our kind has ever known. Ever she thirsted for knowledge, but her lust for even greater understanding drove her to a terrible folly. There was not a creature in the forest beyond the range of her powers, and yet she was not content. Mastering the forms of animals, fish, birds, and serpents was not enough for her, and Agnilla's thoughts finally turned to the insect world.

"No one had ever discovered the secrets of those creatures that creep and buzz, and her heart became inflamed with the desire to learn all she could. From our early beginnings, that branch of lore has been closed to us, and our fore-fathers forbade its study, with good cause.

"It is said that the shape of insects is almost impossible to attain, but that alone is not the reason why the discipline was avoided. Legends spoke of Wergle Masters in the ancient past who dabbled in such experiments and of the horror that befell them. There is great peril wergling into an insect: The mind of a werling alters, and he forgets his former existence.

"That is what happened to Agnilla Hellekin. She had grown proud and considered herself far too skilled to succumb to such hazards; her gift surpassed that of any who had gone before. Yet to ensure her triumph, she…"

Finnen faltered and hastily cleared his throat.

"What did she do?" Liffidia asked.

"Thought she could cheat," the boy answered clumsily as he fumbled to reorganize the story in his head. "And for a while it worked…

"Yes, to begin with, Agnilla's attempts were successful. The first insect she wergled into was a huge and beautiful moth that flew through Hagwood, sailing silently between the trees with the moonlight scattering over her fragmented eyes.

"The other werlings were amazed and honored her as the mightiest that had ever lived. But it did not stop there.

"Too fiercely did the lust for that dreadful knowledge burn within her, and twice more she transformed into insect forms. Then on that third and last time her powers failed her, and she became a monstrous, hybrid terror—part wasp, part spider.

"The other werlings ran to her aid, calling out the unlocking passwords, but they were useless, for the frightful shape that Agnilla had assumed was entirely new, and over it those ancient charms had no control. Desperately they implored her to wergle back, but the previous transformations had afflicted Agnilla without her realizing. Each time, her mind had suffered, and now it was too late. Agnilla Hellekin no longer existed. Her mind and will had fallen into that of the hideous nightmare she had become, and so the greatest of our kind was lost.

"When the werlings realized there was no hope of her redemption, they were forced to drive the vile creature from the wood and out over the Hagburn. There, in the deep forest, behind the holly fence, she made her awful abode, and it is said by some that she dwells there still—Frighty Aggie."

Finnen fell silent and passed a hand over his eyes.

"O Frighty Aggie, sting not me," Gamaliel murmured with a shiver.

Gulping his last mouthful, Tollychook glanced around warily as if he expected the terrible monster to suddenly spring from the gloom.

"Now I understand why Gibble was so angry," Liffidia breathed. "Mother should have told me the story years ago."

"Perhaps she thought you'd had enough nightmares," Finnen said. "What with your father being carried off and all."

The girl eyed him somberly. "It didn't stop your grandmother telling it to you," she replied. "Both your parents are dead, aren't they?"

Finnen hung his head and said no more.

"Woooo—Frighty Aggie!" Mufus Doolan wailed, breaking the sudden tension. "I liked that. I'd love to see that lair of hers."

Bufus jumped to his feet. "Dare you to go to the holly fence!" he cried.

"Do you think we'd spot her from there?" his brother asked.

"Bet we could—and I bet she stinks!"

Finnen raised his eyes and regarded them in annoyance. The story had inspired the Doolans far more than he had anticipated.

"Nobody's going anywhere," he stated firmly. "Especially not to the holly fence. You must never, ever go that way—do you understand?"

The brothers sneered. "S'only a barmy old story, anyway," Mufus moaned. "She'd be long dead by now, even if it was true."

"Oh, it's true all right," Finnen snapped, and the bitterness in his voice startled everyone.

At that moment Tollychook leaped up and frantically pointed over their heads into the wood.

"Look! Look!" he squealed.

A hideous fear gripped the others, and they whirled about. "Sting not me!" Bufus pleaded as he fell on his face.

"What is it?" Finnen hissed, unable to see anything monstrous lurking in the shadowy dark.

Tollychook stared at their frightened faces and in a small, abashed voice muttered, "There's a hedgehog over there."

And so the strained mood was dispelled, and laughing,

the werlings ran from the roots of the ash to where a small prickly shape was ambling through the dead leaves.

Hearing them approach, the urchin rolled into a tight ball and would not budge until Finnen called to it softly and gained its trust. Presently the creature uncurled, and its beady eyes inspected the others before waddling on its way once more.

Deeper into the wood the werlings traveled with their new companion, carefully observing its movements—at times falling on all fours to copy its shambling gait.

The night wore on, and often the hedgehog would pause to snout and sift the leaves with its glistening nose, searching for grubs and beetles. Once it found a large slug, which it chewed happily and stickily for several minutes.

Tollychook had been contemplating a further foray into his provisions, but the sight of the gluey, tarry meal chased that clean from his thoughts.

"Ack!" he exclaimed. "That's disgusting, that be."

Finnen chuckled. "Don't speak too soon," he said, lifting the lantern so that the light fell full upon the last unpleasant morsel. "Sometimes when you've wergled into a shape and stay that way for a while you get the funniest cravings. I've eaten lots of bluebottles."

The children shrieked in revulsion, but the laughter died on Finnen's lips and his face fell.

"Where are they?" he cried, staring this way and that. "How long have they been gone?"

Only then did the others realize that two of their number were missing, but no one had seen them slip away. Mufus and Bufus Doolan were nowhere to be found.

Holding the lantern aloft, Finnen darted into the surrounding dark, calling the brothers' names, but no voices answered.

"When was the last time anyone saw them?" he cried desperately. "Can you remember?"

The others shook their heads. "I heard one of them whisper something two beetles ago," Liffidia said. "I couldn't hear what it was, but didn't think anything of that. They're always muttering to one another."

Finnen rubbed his forehead and tried not to panic. "That can't have been more than an hour since," he calculated. "Maybe less. If we set off right away we might be able to catch up with them."

"What did they run off for?" Tollychook groaned, failing to see the significance of the brothers' disappearance. "The prickly slug chewer's getting away. Spoil everything, them two do."

Gamaliel and Liffidia said nothing; the horrible suspicion that had flared in Finnen's mind had also dawned on them.

"They can't have," Liffidia gasped.

"Yes, they would!" Gamaliel whimpered. "You know what they're like."

Dragging his fingers through his hair, Finnen gave a yell of anger. "Idiots!" he shouted. "What got into them? Are they mad?"

Tollychook fidgeted awkwardly. "Where you think they've gone then?" he mumbled.

"It's obvious," Finnen answered. "The fools have gone to the holly fence—to find Frighty Aggie."

# Chapter 8
# The Lair of Frighty Aggie

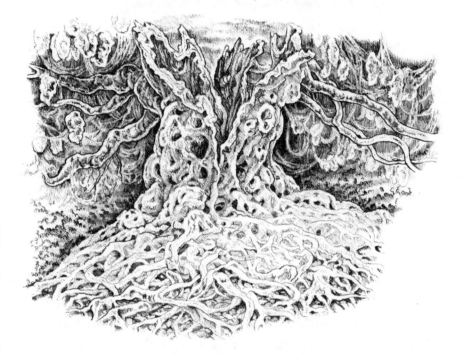

Through the night-wrapped wood the werlings raced, their hearts pounding with fear and dread.

Haring before the others, Finnen wished there had been time to take his charges back to their homes and fetch help, but such a delay might prove fatal for Mufus and Bufus. Yet still he regretted bringing them.

Liffidia could run almost as fast as Finnen, but Tolly-chook was not swift and Gamaliel was only slightly quicker. Vital minutes were constantly squandered while Finnen waited for them to catch up.

Deep into the trees he led them, pressing further than they had ever been, until at last they heard the rushing of water and one by one they came to the Hagburn.

Soon they were all standing upon the steep brink.

Staring down at the stream as he struggled to catch his breath, Gamaliel felt awfully afraid. The reflected light of the lantern sparkled like liquid fire down there, but when he lifted his gaze to the far bank, all was darkness and strangling shadow.

"Do we have to go across?" he murmured.

Tollychook yelped at the very thought of venturing into that untame forest, but they all knew that it was the only way.

"There are plenty of leaning boughs to use as bridges," Finnen said, shining the lantern further downstream. "We must hurry."

Along the mossy edge of the high bank the werlings ran, to where the first of many branches stretched from the far side to their own. It was almost as if the ugly, twisted trees of the forest had been trying to creep stealthily across, and Gamaliel shuddered at the unwelcome notion. Yet into that fearsome realm they were bound to go.

Choosing the widest branch, Finnen scooted to the eastern side and the others followed.

They had left the comfortable land of the werlings be-hind them and were now standing upon a hostile shore. The difference was remarkable and disquieting.

Peering around him, Gamaliel looked at the unfamiliar trees. There was nothing beautiful in any of them. They were grasping, distorted giants that vied against and throttled their neighbors in what was evidently a daily struggle for light. Beneath the contorted boughs the air was stuffy and oppressive, oozing and rolling between the grotesquely proportioned trunks as a turgid black vapor.

"From here on we have to go in the dark." Finnen's voice cut through Gamaliel's thoughts. "I daren't risk a light. There are too many eyes this side of the stream. Keep your sticks handy, but let's hope we won't need them."

Lifting the lantern, he closed its small door. At once the imprisoning bars of night snapped in around them, stifling their senses.

"We mustn't even call out the Doolans' names," Finnen warned. "It's too dangerous for that here."

"But how will we find them?" Liffidia asked.

"Safe and well, hopefully," came the unsettling reply.

Straining their eyes, they picked their way through the tangled forest, tripping over unseen roots and bruising their shins when they fell.

It was a distressing, floundering journey that seemed to take forever in the engulfing murk. Southward they pressed, drawing no ease from the foreign noises of the forest, which all sounded bleak and menacing.

"Surely we should have found them by now?" Liffidia breathed. "I'm starting to doubt if Mufus and Bufus came this way at all. I think they simply got bored and went home."

"Too late to turn back." Finnen spoke in a soft whisper. "We're here."

Rising before them was a wall of solid darkness that towered far above the highest branches and curved deep into the forest, further than their aching eyes could see.

"The holly fence," Gamaliel murmured. "I never dreamed I'd ever look on it, and never wanted to neither."

That dense hedge of holly was a daunting barrier. A fortress built from spiky, leathery leaves and choking, knotted growth, it was a bastion of despair. The sight of it crushed the werlings' spirits utterly.

"Us'll never get through there," Tollychook warbled, glancing up to where the ragged battlements vanished into cavernous shadow.

"Do you really believe Frighty Aggie is still alive?" Gamaliel whispered nervously.

Taking a step closer to the glossy, prickling leaves, Finnen took a few moments to answer. "If she is, then she's right behind this," he said grimly.

"But Mufus and Bufus aren't," Liffidia insisted. "Even if they came this far, they would have turned back. This is an evil place; my skin's crawling. I feel as though a hundred eyes were watching me."

The others agreed. The atmosphere was charged with malice, and from the holly fence there floated a faint reek of death and corruption.

"You're right," Finnen decided. "Let's go back, and quickly. When I catch hold of those two truants…"

Before he could finish, a faint, pitiful cry came echoing from beyond the vast hedge, and the werlings stared at one another in horror.

"They are in there!" Finnen hissed.

Tollychook backed away in terror. "Crickle crackle,

wergle thee, stray not from the cobweb tree," he wailed. "She's eatin' them!"

Finnen rushed forward and frantically sought for a way through the evergreen bulwark. Dropping to his knees, he groped at the tangled stems, battering the sharp leaves aside with his stick.

"I can get in here," he called over his shoulder.

"Wait!" Liffidia urged. "There's nothing you can do against her!"

The anguished cry was sent up once more. It was a ghastly, blood-freezing scream—filled with horror and pain. Wasting no more time, Finnen dived into the gap he had made, and the holly fence swallowed him.

Crouched by the opening, Liffidia knew she could not let him go alone. With her heart in her mouth, she hurried after.

Still singing the childhood rhyme to ward the nightmare of Frighty Aggie away, Tollychook sobbed and Gamaliel felt helpless.

"I can't just stand here waiting!" Gamaliel finally blurted as the seconds dragged by. "Anything might be happening in there."

"Don't you go!" Tollychook begged. "Don't leave me all by meself. That's worse than owt else."

But Gamaliel was already squeezing into the gap, and blubbering dismally, Tollychook followed.

Through the narrow, scratching tunnel of holly they pushed, the shiny leaves jabbing into their faces and snagging their clothes. For many unchecked years the fence had stood, and the breadth of its tangled ramparts had grown very deep.

Barging his way ahead, Finnen was filled with doubt as he steeled himself for the monstrous horror he was about to encounter.

The repulsive stench became stronger, and he nearly yelled when his fingers met a clinging, sticky spider's thread.

He was getting close to the other side. A sickly gray radiance glimmered between the dense leaves in front, and bracing himself for the hideous unknown, he plunged straight through them.

Finnen Lufkin stumbled to a standstill.

A loathsome, eerie scene was unveiled before him. Beyond the mighty barricade of holly stretched a wide clearing. Toward one remote corner the ground rose steadily, and there, thrusting up from that parched mound, was the lair of Frighty Aggie.

It was a huge, black, tortured shape: a massive dead tree whose bark was blighted by disease and blasted by lightning. The crippled boughs corkscrewed their way from one side of the curving hedge to the other, forming the rafters of a misshapen roof, and beneath them the malformed trunk was punctured with dozens of dark and gaping holes.

Cold with fear, Finnen eyed those ominous entrances and swallowed hard. It was a vile, pestiferous place, and death hung heavily about it.

Suddenly Liffidia emerged from the leaves behind him but instantly recoiled.

All around the clearing, looking like macabre and spectral bunting, were swathes of old and filthy webs. Gray, dirt-clogged cords clung to every twisting branch, and the moonlight that filtered through that unclean mesh appeared squalid and foul. Even the sharp stones that surrounded the repulsive tree and its radiating, serpentine roots were smothered by dusty strands. But not all the threads were old and coated with grime; in that ghostly light many were fresh and glistening.

Liffidia cast her gaze higher, and at that moment Gamaliel and Tollychook joined them.

When their eyes adjusted to the ghastly glare, they saw that hanging from the branches were countless cocooned bundles.

None of them had ever felt so afraid. "It's her larder," Gamaliel breathed, feeling sick and faint.

Suspended from slender ropes and bound in suffocating webs were the festering remains of Frighty Aggie's victims. Peering up at the carcasses of her bygone feasts, the werlings could just make out what manner of creatures those bones had once belonged to.

The shriveled bodies of mice and voles formed the most numerous part of the grisly hoard, but here and there they recognized a sparrow's beak or weasel's foot sticking from a slightly larger parcel, and the dried corpse of a frog could easily be discerned. All the captured prey of Frighty Aggie was here. She kept it dangling from the branches until her insect mind deemed it ripe and ready for her awful jaws.

"Sucked the goodness clean out of 'em all," Tollychook wept.

But there were bigger creatures caught in Aggie's nets. Gamaliel saw the mask of a badger grinning down at him, and he tried not to think what had become of the rest of the hapless beast.

Wrenching his gaze away, Finnen searched for any sign of Mufus and Bufus, but the brothers were nowhere to be seen in that disgusting domain. Anxiously he wondered if they had been dragged into one of those holes in the tree and were even now being devoured in the dark.

A mournful shriek suddenly threw his sinister suspicions aside, and finally they all saw where those cries originated.

Across the clearing, partly concealed by festooning webs, was a fox cub. Trussed tightly, it was hanging upside down, its eyes rolling in terror.

Another mewling call escaped its jaws when it beheld once more the frightful thing suspended nearby, and realizing what it was, Tollychook retched and looked away.

Swinging slowly upon a silvery string, like some grisly pendulum, was a second cub, but it was dead and half eaten. The constricting bonds were splashed with blood, and the ground beneath was stained and spattered.

Finnen pushed the others back against the holly fence.

"The Doolans were never here," he muttered. "We have to go."

Liffidia shook her head. "But that poor fox is still alive," she declared. "I'm not abandoning it here to be eaten." And before anyone could stop her she darted forward.

"Come back!" Finnen gasped. "This is madness!"

But Liffidia was determined. Leaping over the thick, ropelike roots that broke the surface of that stony ground, she ran to the other side of the clearing—to where the fox cub was twirling woefully.

Imprisoned in Aggie's snares, the animal gave a feeble twitch when it saw her approach, and its amber, fear-filled eyes fixed beseechingly upon her.

"Be calm now," she called softly, avoiding the red stains on the ground. "I'll rescue you."

Finnen could not believe what she was doing. So far they had been incredibly lucky and had seen nothing of Frighty Aggie, but he did not expect their miraculous good fortune to last.

"We don't have time for this," he mumbled. So, leaving Tollychook and Gamaliel behind, he ran to fetch her back.

Gamaliel turned to look at the deformed tree with its many dark holes, and he trembled, fumbling with the absurdly inadequate stick in his hands.

Standing beneath the trapped cub, Liffidia wondered how to release it. The creature was not dangling high off the ground. Its furry, web-wrapped face was almost level with her own, and she held out her hand in a gesture of friendship and trust.

The fox cub licked her palm then gave a forsaken whine that pierced her heart. Liffidia looked up at the suspending thread. It did not appear to be very strong; perhaps if she wrenched at it....

Leaping up, the werling girl caught hold of the binding cords to yank the animal free, but Aggie's silks were stronger than they appeared and did not yield. Then, to her dismay, Liffidia discovered that her hands were held fast to the cocoon. She, too, was captured.

"I'm stuck!" she cried as Finnen came running. "The webs are like glue! I can't get my hands loose!"

Grasping her wrists, Finnen pulled fiercely, but it made no difference. The petrified fox let out a grievous yowl.

"Keep it quiet!" Finnen begged her. "I don't like this; she should have shown herself by now."

"What am I to do?" Liffidia cried, panicking.

With a wary glance at the monster's hideous abode,

Finnen let go of the girl's wrists and stepped away from her. Then, throwing off his coat, he raised his arms and at once wergled into a woodpecker.

Up the bird flew, up to where the tip of the cub's tail poked from the sticky bindings and the suspending strand stretched into the overhanging branches.

In one swift, scissoring movement, the woodpecker's beak attacked the cord and snipped it in two.

Liffidia fell backward and the fox cub tumbled on top of her.

Down Finnen swooped, wergling into a stoat whose sharp claws set to work immediately.

From the fox's body the tight, ensnaring webs were torn. Too frail to bark with joy, the young animal could only wheeze its gratitude while Liffidia wiped the filthy stuff from her hands.

Watching them from the hedge, Gamaliel and Tollychook almost cheered.

"Wait till we tell Master Gibble what Finnen did this night!" Gamaliel said proudly.

"Won't Mufus and Bufus be amazed when they learn where we been?" Tollychook declared, patently thinking that the danger was over and they were safe.

But the real peril was just beginning.

THE fox cub could not walk; it had spent too long tied and bound. All the strength had left its legs and it could not even stand. Every time the poor creature attempted to raise itself from the floor, it staggered and collapsed.

Liffidia tried to help, but it was no use.

"Do you think we could carry it?" she asked when Finnen returned to his normal shape.

The boy was not listening. He was even more uneasy and afraid than before.

Staring at the bloodstained ground, he noticed that it had not completely seeped into the dry soil.

In a small, scared voice he murmured, "We interrupted her...Frighty Aggie was feeding when we got here. She must have heard us and slunk away."

"Where to?" Liffidia breathed.

Only then did Finnen see a trail of dark red splashes leading from the mire beneath the fox's dead sibling. Crimson droplets sprinkled the stones, heading toward the tree, until suddenly the dribbles ceased and at last he knew. The gory marks had spilled from Aggie's jaws, and the trail plainly showed that she never returned to her lair—she had climbed into the branches above.

"Run!" he yelled sharply. "Leave the fox and run—as fast as you can—back to the hedge!"

Liffidia did not understand what had happened. Finnen looked terrified.

Gamaliel and Tollychook did not know what had come over him, either. Frantically they stared at the blighted tree, but all the entrances were still dark and empty. They did not know that directly behind them a single, glistening thread was steadily descending.

"Do as I tell you!" Finnen was shouting at Liffidia. "Leave it. We don't have much time!"

The girl shoved him away from her. "I won't!" she retorted. "I'll get the others to help me if you're too selfish." Spinning around to face the holly fence, she prepared to call out to Gamaliel and Tollychook, but the plea instantly became a horrified scream.

At once Gamaliel and Tollychook whirled about and at last they saw it: the nightmare that haunted the dark dreams of werling infants, the cradle horror who plagued their nights and dwelt in deep, fear-drowned corners—Frighty Aggie.

Down the silvery rope she had stealthily been creeping, but now those noisy morsels were aware of her and squealing shrilly, as did every wriggling meal. Not waiting to scale the remaining distance, Frighty Aggie pounced.

She was the most abhorrent vision that any of the werlings had ever conceived. The ancient monster of their kind was harrowing beyond measure and, in the ages since she had been driven over the Hagburn, had grown immense in size.

A frightful fusion of wasp and spider, her bloated body was a livid, poisonous yellow, striped by ugly black bands. Eight enormous jointed legs arched high over her large swiveling head, where baneful, clustering eyes bulged with greed.

Onto the ground she leaped, and her jaws clicked feverishly together as she bore down upon Gamaliel and Tollychook.

In one hideous moment it was over.

Shrieking, Kernella's brother was flung to the floor and Tollychook slammed against the stones beside him.

Over their bodies the apparition crawled, the ragged feathers of her antennae sweeping across their cringing faces as she trussed them in her clinging cords.

The werlings were held fast, and when they struggled,

the webs constricted and bound them even tighter. Tolly-chook bawled despairingly, but there was no escape.

As soon as they were securely imprisoned, Frighty Aggie turned her malignant attention on those others who had dared to raid her sweet pantry.

At the far side of the infernal clearing, transfixed by the spectacle of that abominable scourge, Finnen and Liffidia could only stand and gape as it wheeled about upon those monstrous legs and came galloping toward them.

Over the iron-hard ground the fiend came ravening, her talons clattering on the stones as she lunged for the stricken werlings.

Pale and aghast, they beheld her awful speed and saw the many eyes glittering foully.

The fox cub howled. Then, at the last moment, as the shadow of Frighty Aggie fell upon them, Finnen shook himself.

Snatching up a large stone, he hurled it at the lunging head and an outraged screech issued from the virulent jaws. The countless eyes turned on him, but Finnen darted from her and a second stone bounced off her horny hide.

Aggie pursued him. She would feast upon that dainty first of all, and savor each drop of its impertinent blood.

Luring the frightful adversary away from Liffidia and the fox cub, Finnen sped to the center of the clearing, but Aggie's eight legs carried her swiftly, and he realized it was impossible to outrun her. He had to keep her occupied so that the others could escape, and so, when the chill shadow engulfed him, he knew there was only one thing he could do.

At once he wergled into a shrew.

The terrible jaws came snapping down, but instead of

fleeing from her, the shrew raced between her talons and scuttled beneath that venom-gorged belly.

Aggie reared in fury and spun around in a rage, but the shrew hid from her evil glance and nipped in and out of her legs, constantly avoiding those glittering eyes. The monster was compelled to clatter in a revolving circle, seeking the shrew that evaded her.

A bubbling hiss spewed from her jaws as she vainly tried to seize him. But Finnen was too nimble, and though the stench of her foul flesh screamed in his nostrils, he endured it stoically.

Liffidia could not bear to watch. Never had a werling done a braver or more valiant deed. But Finnen would not be able to dodge the nightmare forever. Springing across to where Tollychook and Gamaliel were still squirming in their cocoons, Liffidia tore a large holly leaf from the hedge.

Not daring to touch the sticky webs with her hands, she used the holly's sharp spikes to rip through the clinging bonds.

When their arms and legs were freed, Gamaliel and Tollychook staggered to their feet. They stared at Frighty Aggie, still reeling in the drunken dance that Finnen's shrew obliged her to perform.

But now the monster was jabbing the ground furiously with her sting, and to the werlings' dismay, they realized that Finnen was tiring.

Scudding through the gigantic, trampling legs, the shrew was not as quick as before. While they watched, Finnen was nearly caught by the dreadful point of the lethal sting, but he swerved awkwardly aside and the dry earth was speared with her pounding malice.

"He's not going to last much longer!" Liffidia cried.

"What shall us do?" Tollychook blubbered. "What shall us do?"

Retrieving his stick from the ground where it had fallen, Gamaliel brandished it fiercely.

"We've got to help him," he shouted, and waving the pathetic weapon over his head, he rushed to attack Frighty Aggie—yelling at the top of his voice.

Beneath the yellow and black bands of the nightmare's cankerous belly, the shrew ducked and dodged. Finnen's limbs ached and he knew the end would be soon. Downward pumped the sting, and black poison squirted over the surrounding stones. Finnen leaped forward but he was too slow; a great talon came sweeping from nowhere and he was knocked sideways.

Thrown across the ground, the shrew saw a glimpse of the noxious creature bearing down upon him, and then it was finished. As he sprawled on the parched soil, one of the savage, hooked claws came knifing from above, and the cruel tip drove deep into his flesh, pinning him to the ground.

Finnen shrieked in pain. So great was his agony that the shrew shape vanished and there he lay, the fiend's claw skewering his right arm.

Slavering putrid fluids, Aggie lowered her jaws and they clacked together eagerly. Staring up at the calamitous horror, Finnen closed his eyes.

"Get off him!" Gamaliel screeched suddenly. "Let him be!"

With all his might he brought the stick cracking down against the enemy's black-and-yellow body.

Keeping her victim pinned to the ground, the repugnant creature lifted her malignant head and turned.

Liffidia and Tollychook had already joined Gamaliel, and they, too, were assailing her ulcerous bulk.

Against that tough hide, their blows were futile; nevertheless, they were an irritating distraction that had to be dealt with.

Spinning about, she confronted them, and Tollychook immediately dropped his weapon at the sight of that awful countenance.

A gurgling snarl echoed in her dark throat and she lashed out viciously.

Another of her great claws punched Tollychook in the stomach, and he screamed when it flicked him into the air. Catapulted off his feet, his plump figure was sent flying. He hurtled up into the branches, where he was instantly entangled in the thick webs and could not get down.

The others could do nothing to save him.

In desperation Gamaliel clouted one of the gargantuan legs, but the stick splintered upon that adamantine shell and flew apart in his hands.

Only Liffidia's frantic efforts inflicted any injury to that rancorous foe. When the dark head came swinging around, she brought her stick crashing into a cluster of eyes, and a bitter screech blasted from the fetid jaws.

It was the first true pain that Frighty Aggie had suffered in an age and more. Incensed and boiling with murderous wrath, she rounded upon the werling girl and dashed the weapon from her hands before throwing her off balance.

Liffidia fell back, and the apparition towered over her, ranging itself around so that its stinking body lifted above her head and the evil sting pulsed in readiness to strike.

Down it lunged and Liffidia threw up her hands.

Seeing her plight, Gamaliel gave a shout and leaped forward—straight into the hideous sting's path.

The lethal spike descended, crushing him to his knees. He squealed in agony when the atrocity stabbed into his shoulder.

Deeply bit the unholy sting, and when Aggie heaved herself up once more, it tore from her body.

Into Gamaliel's veins her pollution pumped, and a cold blackness exploded within him. The color drained from his face and he collapsed—senseless and deathly still.

"Gamaliel!" Liffidia cried, but she could not reach him, for already another sting was pushing from the nightmare's body. Frighty Aggie prepared to strike her.

Speared beneath the claw, Finnen heard the shrieks of his friends and roused himself for one final effort.

Using all his fading strength, he strained hard and changed his shape into that of a rat with long, razor-sharp teeth.

Twisting round, he lifted his head and clamped his incisors about the apparition's claw.

The horny shell was hard as flint but it was not impregnable. A revolting "CRACK!" rang out in the clearing, and the rat's teeth crunched clean through the talon, shearing it off completely.

Profane screams galed from Aggie's throat. Dark green blood came frothing from the truncated limb and gushed, steaming, upon the ground.

Gagging on the odious taste, the rat slumped onto the stones. His last spark of energy quenched, Finnen wergled back into his usual shape. There was no hope left.

Frighty Aggie's curdling screech became a vengeful

babbling, and she stood over Finnen's prostrate form, her eyes blazing with hatred.

The loathly head bent down, and Finnen felt her hot, reeking breath beat on him. Turning his face in disgust, he waited for the death blow, but it never came.

Over his wincing features, the ragged antennae raked, and a purling gargle sounded behind the clicking jaws. The werling's flesh rebelled at her defiling touch, and a wild, impossible thought ignited in his mind—the monster was smelling him.

"Kill me and have done!" he yelled.

A pale, luminous light flickered in Frighty Aggie's searching eyes when the probing antennae groped at and caressed a small leather bag attached to the werling's belt. Then, to Finnen's consternation and revulsion, a thin, mocking laugh floated down to him.

It was a scathing, awful sound that rent the shadows and set the cobwebbed bundles of her rotting larder jiggling on their strings.

With that, to Finnen's bewilderment, she left him.

Back over the stony ground the horrendous creature crept, her baleful eyes trained intently upon him. In slow, measured steps she withdrew, and her cold, creaking laughter echoed across that drear, death-plagued place. Up the mound the giant spider legs crawled, leaving a trail of sizzling ooze in her wake.

Finnen gritted his teeth and tugged the severed claw from his arm. Clutching at the wound, he raised his head, just in time to see Frighty Aggie haul her vile bulk into one of the diseased tree's many dark holes. With a final, rattling laugh, the horror vanished.

There was no time to ponder on what had happened and why she had departed at the very moment of her victory. Confused and weary, Finnen stumbled to his feet and staggered across to where Liffidia was kneeling beside Gamaliel.

The girl lifted her head at the sound of his approach, and her cheeks were streaked with tears.

"I...I think he's dead." She wept.

The fox cub began to howl again.

# Chapter 9
# Stewing Roots

amaliel Tumpin was gray and cold. The brutal sting was still embedded in his shoulder, its poison sac pumping hideously.

Finnen crouched beside him and gazed on the youngster's ashen face. Even as he looked, the grayness of Gamaliel's flesh became tinged with a foul green pallor that intensified with every spasm of the pulsing venom.

Angrily Finnen reached out to draw the vile sting from his dead friend's body.

Suddenly a stern, unfamiliar voice shouted.

"Don't be a fool, boy!"

The werlings spun around to see a tall, shadowy figure come crashing into the clearing.

"Are you so ignorant of the werhag's ways?" it demanded.

"Who are you?" Finnen yelled. "Keep away!"

The stranger stepped closer. He was four times the height of the werlings, but Finnen rose to confront him.

"You'll not be much use in a fight with that poor arm of yours now," the newcomer said gruffly.

Finnen glared at him. "I said stay back!" he cried.

The stranger pulled a small knife from his belt and sprang forward. Pushing both werlings out of the way, he raised the blade above Gamaliel's body and plunged it into his flesh.

Liffidia shrieked and flew at him, but it was Finnen who pulled her off.

"Wait," he told her. "Look what he's doing."

Startled, the girl watched as the knife sliced a red circle in Gamaliel's shoulder, deftly carving out a chunk of flesh in which the sting was impaled.

A leathery hand was then clamped over the hollow wound and Frighty Aggie's ghastly weapon was flung away in disgust.

The newcomer returned his attention to the werlings, and a solemn smile appeared in his grizzled beard.

"You'll forgive Smith's ill manners," he excused himself. "But there weren't no time for soft speech. If you'd pulled that accursed tickler from your little friend, he'd be well dead by now."

Liffidia and Finnen gazed at the Wandering Smith in astonishment. The Pucca's brilliant green eyes gleamed out beneath his thick, woolly brows, and for a brief moment their fears and the memory of terror faded.

"What do you mean?" Finnen asked when the sensation passed. "Are you saying Gamaliel's still alive?"

The Smith touched Gamaliel's forehead. "Barely," he answered. "But this is not the place to administer healing. No more can the Smith do in this benighted stink hole. The tiny fellow is not free of the danger yet, for death has entered in and maybe it will not leave him."

Carefully picking Gamaliel from the ground, the Smith strode back across the clearing to the great hole he had made in the holly fence.

"Smith has pitched his camp a way yonder," he told them, sweeping the fox cub up in his other arm. "He can do more for your companion there."

Finnen and Liffidia glanced at each other. They did not know who or what this person was, yet they were only too glad to leave this abominable domain behind them. Nursing his own wound, Finnen began to hurry after the Pucca, but Liffidia hesitated.

"What is it?" Finnen called.

"Aren't we forgetting something?" she asked pointedly.

Finnen frowned, then gasped when he realized.

High above them a forlorn voice wailed.

"Heeeeeelp! Get me down!"

"Tollychook!" Finnen cried.

Still snared in the dirty, festooning webs, poor Tollychook sniveled miserably.

Hearing the plaintive call, the Smith turned and chuckled at Tollychook's predicament.

"Thimbleglaive," he commanded. "Fly up and be the sword. Cut away both web and cord!"

From its sheath the little knife came shooting. Up into

the branches it spun, cleaving a glittering arc in the dismal air.

Seeing the magical blade come rushing toward him, Tollychook scrunched up his face and braced himself.

Into Frighty Aggie's clinging nets the knife went, slashing and hacking at incredible speed, cutting them from the astonished and frightened werling.

Suddenly Tollychook lurched downward as the last remaining threads were severed. He tumbled from the branches like a falling apple.

He landed on the hard ground with a terrific bump, but he was too relieved to be out of the filthy cobwebs to yelp.

"Thimbleglaive!" the Smith called. "Home!"

The knife rocketed from above and slid back into its sheath.

"If that's the last of your party," the Pucca said, nodding at Tollychook, "we'd best get gone." And he strode into the hedge, leaving the others to hasten after.

Finnen was the last to follow, but before he entered the high tunnel, he looked one last time upon the lair of Frighty Aggie.

Within one of those dark gaping holes he thought he caught a glimpse of her many eyes regarding him keenly. Again he heard that chilling, sinister laugh, and running after his friends, he finally suspected why the nightmarish creature had spared him.


ONCE more the werlings ventured into the forest, but they did not have far to travel. The Wandering Smith was camped only a short distance away, and presently they saw the merry flames of his small fire crackling through the trees ahead.

Soon they were warming themselves by its heartening heat while the Pucca tended to Gamaliel's shoulder.

Laying the pale werling upon a bed of furs, he muttered strange words over the wound and pressed iron charms against the poisoned flesh. Taking a small leather bottle from the cart that was standing close by, he poured three drops of the bright blue liquid it contained into the raw sinew, and sang softly under his breath.

The others watched him apprehensively, but they no longer feared or were suspicious of him.

While they waited, Liffidia fed the fox cub some warm milk that the Smith had given her, and the half-starved animal nuzzled lovingly against her.

Brushing the last waving wisps of web from his sleeves, Tollychook gazed around them. He stared curiously at the Smith's handcart.

It was a rickety, much-battered contraption that had tagged along behind the Wandering Smith for many years and miles. But it was the contents that fascinated Tollychook.

With the covers removed, the Smith's wares glinted and glowed in the firelight. There were iron pots, long shapely ladles, a collection of swords, knives, goblets, metal helms similar to the one the Pucca wore, steel collars, a kettle whose spout was shaped like a leaping fish. Fire-blackened pans, copper lanterns pierced with hundreds of tiny holes, a cowbell, plates of tin, a wooden chest containing a wealth of talismans and amulets like those he wore about his neck and had used upon Gamaliel. Over the side of the cart, a vast array of spoons of various sizes hung upon a length of wire, and their many shallow bowls appeared to dance and brim with flame.

Yet in among that abundance Tollychook saw other things that he did not like the look of: small bronze statues with fearsome faces, effigies of ancient forest gods and fire devils.

"That's as much as the Smith can do," the Pucca said, applying a poultice to Gamaliel's shoulder. "Should draw out more of the werhag's venom, but only time will decree if he lives or dies."

The werlings looked at Gamaliel, and it seemed to them that already the deathly pallor had left his face.

Liffidia smiled up at the Pucca and thanked him warmly. "We are always told not to have any dealings with big folk," she said. "I don't know why. Are they all as kind as you?"

He merely laughed in reply and began examining Finnen's injury.

"Are you from the Hollow Hill?" she asked.

A frown clouded the Smith's face, but he said nothing.

In brooding silence he bandaged Finnen's arm, and Liffidia was left wondering if she had offended him.

"Is this whole forest and the stream named after Frighty Aggie?" Tollychook piped up suddenly. "You called her the werhag."

Placing Finnen's arm in a sling, the Smith settled himself before the fire. "There's more than one hag in Hagwood," he muttered darkly.

The werlings looked at one another, feeling uncomfortable and not sure what to say. Meanwhile, the Pucca hung a large covered pot over the flames. Leaning against the bole of a gnarled tree, he regarded them for a long time before uttering another word.

A thread of steam began to curl from beneath the pot lid, and Tollychook's nose wrinkled with pleasure at the delicious smell.

Liffidia and Finnen suddenly realized that they were famished, but their packs had been left on the other side of the holly fence, together with the lantern.

"Root stew," the Smith finally said, rising from his seat and doling the bubbling food onto the smallest plates he could find in his cart. The plates were still very large and cumbersome for the werlings to handle, but they accepted them with gratitude. "Not a banquet," he admitted, "but it fills a hole when your belly's wagging."

The children ate the food hungrily. The stew was boiling hot, and Tollychook burned his tongue, but he huffed and blew and gobbled it down. The taste was unlike anything the werlings were accustomed to, containing many unfamiliar herbs and odd-looking tubers chopped into chunks, but it was still more than acceptable, and even more welcome after the trials of the night.

Their host, however, ate only a couple of mouthfuls before sighing and setting his portion upon the ground. "Mutton stew old Smith was hoping for last night," he remarked sadly. "But there was no light in the farmhouse window, aye, and no farmer neither."

The brilliant green of his eyes glimmered while he watched the werlings clear their plates, and his woolly brows crept together as a secret thought flickered in his mind.

Chewing the last spoonful, Finnen caught the strange look on the Pucca's face.

"Smith had forgotten about the little changers who live on the border of the forest," he murmured, more to himself than to the others. "Maybe he's not the only one. Easy to slip from memories, they are. Would you risk it, Smith—should you risk it?"

"Any more?" Tollychook ventured, peering hopefully at the pot.

The Smith stirred himself and dished out the last of the stew.

"Well, my jolly friends," he said brightly. "What sport were you playing with the warden of the holly? Deadly work that is, too grim for the likes of you is she. Lucky that the Smith heard your hullabalooing. This side of the stream is no place for your kind to be adventuring."

Finnen explained what had led them there, and when the tale was complete, the Pucca fingered his beard.

"Not like the werhag to leave her prey like that," he muttered. "Smith has never heard it happen. What was it about you she found not to her taste?"

The boy could not answer and lowered his gaze.

"Soon as you've rested," the Pucca said, changing the subject, "and the hours have judged what will befall your stung companion, the Smith will guide you home. But hearken to these words and heed his warning—never set foot inside the wild forest again."

"That I won't!" Tollychook declared emphatically.

"Keep to your own trees," the Smith continued. "Ages have you spent hiding from sight, ignored and over-looked—let that way endure."

Finnen felt vaguely uneasy. "You speak as though there was more to fear in the forest than we already know," he said.

The green eyes glinted. "There is," he answered bleakly. "Hagwood is a treacherous corner of the wild world. Trust no one; shun those not of your race."

"Even folk like you?" Liffidia asked.

"There are no others like Smith," he told her sharply. "Not no more, not hereabouts."

Glancing quickly at the night-shrouded branches above, as if searching for something, the Pucca whispered, "Most important of all, have no dealings with those who dwell in the Hollow Hill. If you value your lives and those you love."

"We never see the likes of them," Tollychook chirped, happily stroking his full tummy. "But I never heard nowt bad against 'em."

"I don't think the hillmen even know we exist," Finnen added.

The Smith snorted and pointed a grimy finger at each of them. "Wer-rats," he proclaimed. "That was their name for you in days long gone. Whether they still recall you... Smith was just wondering that himself."

"You do come from the Hollow Hill, don't you?" Liffidia said shrewdly.

The Pucca grunted.

"Say rather that Smith did—once," he replied. "But that was so many springs ago, when the forest was called Dunrake and the crown graced the brow of a king."

Tollychook whistled. "I never heard any tale about no king," he said.

"What happened to make you leave?" Finnen asked.

The Smith considered for a moment. How much could he tell? Indeed, should he draw them any further into his confidence? Merely by talking with them he had endangered their lives. Did he have the right to compound that hazard any further?

"Ain't no pretty story," he said at last. "A black history full of spite and malice, and only one other knows the full truth of it besides Smith. You'll not sleep the easier for the hearing, and shadows will seem darker when it's done. Be very sure before you open your ears."

The werlings looked uncertain. Perhaps it was too great a burden for them. Could he have misjudged them? They were only a small, insignificant people after all, no match for the enemy.

"Shall Smith tell it or no?" he asked, and again he spoke more to himself than to the others.

"Yes, please!" an unexpected voice cried. "Please tell us!"

The werlings whipped around and broke into astonished laughter. There, sitting up on the furs, the color already back in his cheeks, was Gamaliel Tumpin.

Dark rings circled his eyes and he looked a trifle groggy, but otherwise he was back to his old self again and eager for a story of the hillfolk.

The Pucca regarded him and the others afresh. These little people were more hardy than he had surmised, and so finally he made his decision.

Leaving his place by the fire, he refreshed Gamaliel's poultice. Then, taking the velvety wergle pouch in his fingers, he looked at it thoughtfully before chortling and sitting down once more.

"So be it," he began. "Know then the saga of tears and how the tyrant ascended the throne...

"Once, in former, carefree times, in the reign of Ragallach—king of the summer country beneath the Hollow Hill—the Smith worked in the royal forge. He was not alone. Eight other Puccas of greater skill than his own labored there also. To shoe the royal steeds with silver and fashion bright armor for the goblin knights was their chief toil, and their work had no rival.

"Yet other things they made—toys for the royal children: the princesses, Morthanna and Clarisant, and the young prince, Alisander. Cunning and magical were those gimcracks, wrought from precious metals and set with gems. Those were merry years.

"But children grow, even in the underground realm, and the toys grew also. For Prince Alisander the Puccas fashioned the most lovely of all their works: a gold and silver dagger whose haft was fashioned from shimmering crystal. The prince valued it above all the treasures in his father's vaults.

"But as the years crawled by, the mood within the court altered.

"The Lady Morthanna had flowered into the fairest maiden ever to grace the hidden kingdom, yet ambition blazed within her. She yearned for power, but her dreams were in vain, for Alisander was the heir, not she.

"Still she plotted. When a suitor came to woo her, his heart turned instead to Clarisant. Affronted, Morthanna hatched a terrible vengeance, but the lovers disappeared from court. No one ever discovered what befell them.

"Henceforth the realm of King Ragallach became a solemn and mournful place, devoid of song and merriment.

"Yet ever resentment seethed within the Lady Morthanna. Her whispered lies turned friend against friend, and the nobles were set at odds and divided. Dissension and mistrust blossomed in every hall, but from whence the ill humors and deceits came, none could guess. So it continued until the mood soured to the correct degree for Morthanna's designs.

"Upon that dark, grievous day, she came to the forge, charging the nine Puccas to create a small golden casket with an enchanted lock that could only ever be opened by one key and one alone. A gift to her father she claimed it was, and so that no word of its making should reach his ears, the smiths were sworn to secrecy.

"Loving their lord, the Puccas poured all their skill into the building of the glittering box, and when it was completed, Morthanna seized it greedily."

The Smith paused and stared into the depths of the leaping flames as though recalling the heats of the smithy all those years ago. His eyes sparkled and were wet.

"What happened?" Liffidia asked.

"Black deeds," he replied.

"That very night King Ragallach and his guards were slain. Their throats were cut, and the instrument of their murder was the prince Alisander's crystal-handled dagger. The heir to the throne was taken, and so treacherous was the mood that none heeded his pleas of innocence.

"Awaiting the pronouncement of his doom, the prince contrived his escape but was hunted through the forest by the Redcaps and spriggans, who shot at him with spears and arrows dipped in poison.

"Over the heathland Alisander fled, in order to reach the Lonely Mere, for his pursuers despised the touch of water. Yet even as he leaped from the shore, an arrow plunged into his back and he sank, lifeless, into the cold deeps.

"So at last did Morthanna succeed to the throne, and she took to herself the name Rhiannon—High Queen."

Gamaliel caught his breath. "The High Lady!" he cried, interrupting. "But I thought the hillfolk were grand and wonderful."

"She killed her own father?" Liffidia asked, mortified. "Then she let her brother take the blame and die because of it! How could she, how could anyone?"

Shaking his head, the Smith sucked in the air through his teeth. "Many evils were committed in that accursed time," he hissed. "Because Alisander's dagger had been forged in the royal smithy, Rhiannon decreed that Ragallach's blood stained the hands of its makers also. To the forge the wild Redcaps went, shrieking, and slaughtered all they found. Over their own anvils the Puccas were cruelly put to death. Their hands were chopped from their wrists and their heads hacked from their necks. Yet only eight of their number did they slay; the ninth they could not and never did find."

Awestruck, the werlings stared at him.

"Why have you come back?" Finnen asked.

A somber smile split the Pucca's graying beard. "Smith has a task left undone," he said. "A moment ago the little maid inquired as to how Morthanna, the faithless and despised, could be so wholly evil as to murder her own father. This then is the secret that she thought no one else would discover, but Smith got to the root of it.

"Of all the folk in that summer land beneath the turf,

he alone doubted the fair mask of the eldest princess and suspected her true nature. When the suitor came, it was Smith who warned him against her. Then, when the casket of gold was made and she bore it away—Smith followed her, and this is what he learned.

"Down a steeply winding stair she ran, a wicked laugh ever on her lips. Far beneath the earth she descended, to the deepest and most secure of her father's strong rooms. Stout and barred was the door to that dank chamber, and Smith could not presume to know what she did therein. Yet her voice rang faint through the timbers, and his beard curled to hear the dreadful spells it recited. Instructed by the troll witches who once dwelt in the cold hills, Morthanna had become a mistress of filthy arts. Smith shrank into the shadows, covering his ears to blot out the hated words.

"Long he cowered there, but at last the door swung open and out she strode. Harder than diamond was her face, for the foul enchantments had removed any lingering doubt and scruple, and she was now wholly cold and cruel.

"Taking the great key that hung from her waist, she locked the strong room behind her and clasped in her hands the prince's dagger, which she had stolen that day. Then, with murder on her mind, she ran up the stair and headed straight for her father's bedchamber.

"From the unlit corner the Smith crawled, and to the sealed door he inched in fear. What lay beyond it he dared not guess, but he had to know. Putting his mouth to the lock, he spoke a charm that sprang the hasp aside, for it had been made by his own hand and yielded to his pleas.

"Into the chamber the Smith stole.

"It was vast and empty, save for a circle of stones at its

center, and there upon the floor was the golden casket and its key.

"Hands shaking, Smith looked within and howled in revolt. In that moment he should have showed his mettle and done the one deed that would have saved them all, but his stomach rebelled and he could not.

"Instead, he took the casket and fled from the hill. Even as he ran into the trees he heard the horns sounding, announcing the death of the king, but, alas, the Smith thought that they pronounced his own doom. In blind panic he concealed the golden box and went not into the forest again.

"When he uncovered the truth it was too late. The Lady Morthanna had claimed the throne and, as Rhiannon, wields great power. A tyrant She is now, and all Her subjects fear Her."

"That be a thumpin' horrible story," Tollychook burbled.

A corner of the Pucca's mouth lifted in a wry smile. "Tyrant She may be," he added with a gruff chuckle. "And though She has gained all Her desires, not once throughout these long years has She been able to enjoy Her reign. Doubt and dread sit beside Her upon that throne, for Smith stole the casket and She has hunted for it ever since. Until it is found and in Her keeping, not an instant's peace or rest shall She have."

The Pucca's smile broadened in his beard. "How She has searched," he laughed. "A thief Herself She has become, burgling the mounds of ancient chieftains, tearing crowns from the skulls of sleeping kings, but all for naught, all for naught."

"What was in the box?" Gamaliel begged, unable to contain his curiosity any longer.

The smile vanished. The green light flickered beneath the brows and the Pucca's voice sank to a chilling whisper.

"Within that casket," he said, "lies the only hope of destroying the cruel monarch of the Hollow Hill. Therein is Her one fatal weakness. It alone can bring an end to Her immortal life, and that is why, waking and sleeping, Rhiannon is fearful.

"For this is what Smith saw, that evil day in the deep places of the earth when he turned the enchanted key and lifted the glittering lid. This he saw and the memory freezes his bones still. Inside the box, pulsing and beating by loathsome craft—was Rhiannon's very own heart."

A heavy silence fell about the campfire, and the werlings shivered in spite of the flames.

High above, in the topmost branches of the tree that leaned over their heads, a large barn owl blinked its golden eyes then spread its wings. Into the night it flew.

"What was that?" the Pucca said, staring about them. "Smith felt eyes upon him, aye, and ears, too. Hagwood is full of watchful spies."

Rising, he doused the fire and kicked the drowned ashes.

"Come, little changers," he announced. "You must return to your own safer land. Smith will take you."

Quickly he packed the handcart, and took Gamaliel and the fox cub in his arms.

"Soonest you are back in your trees Smith will be happy," he said, striding from the camp. "There is much to do this night. The casket must be removed from the hiding place and then Smith will finish this business by doing what he should have done down in the strong room. Come dawn, Hagwood will be free of the High Lady's tyranny. Hasten, little friends. The night is not yet ended; there still may be many dangers ahead—for us all."

Into the shadows the werlings hurried, but not one of them realized just how deadly that night would prove. Before morning, one of them would be slain.

# CHAPTER 10
# Murder by Moonlight

Upon the barren heath, Mufus and Bufus were enjoying themselves immensely.

As soon as they slipped away from the others, they had run to this empty wasteland, giggling and sniggering at their own sly cleverness.

Wergling into mice, they charged through the coarse grasses that covered the heath, reveling in the freedom of that vast deserted space. Neither of them had ever known such liberty, and to be away from the constant presence of trees was an experience that never ceased to thrill them.

For more than an hour they played in the moonlit dark, discovering the countless pits and shafts that grinned in the expansive scrubland. In high squeaking voices they joked and laughed, mostly at the expense of those they had left behind.

Finally, when they had rampaged as wildly and as reck-lessly as their rodents' legs could manage, they threw them-selves into the long grass where their clothes were heaped in an untidy pile and stared up at the stars while they panted and regained their breath.

Looking for all the world like two relaxing, reclining mice, lounging upon their backs, they lay there, exhausted and content.

It was Mufus who recovered sufficiently to speak first.

"Wish it was like this all the time." He sighed, snapping a grass stem and nibbling it. "Dunno why they make us plod about in groups. Never learn nothin' that way, what with stupid Gammy holdin' us up and that Liffy girl whin-ing about fur pullin' every chance she gets."

His brother grunted his agreement.

"Don't forget Chookface," Bufus said. "With his 'nor-mous feet and guzzlin' all the time."

"Useless bunch."

"Except Lufkin, though. Right clever he is."

Mufus tittered. "Not clever enough to stop us running off," he crowed.

"Know what his trouble is…," Bufus added after a mo-ment's deliberation. "Too soft. Might be a grand wergler, but a pushover all the same. No point bein' smart if you're weak with it. Nah, you and me, we're the best of that sorry lot."

"What do you reckon they're doin' right this minute?"

Bufus lifted himself up on all fours and began an exaggerated waddle. "Here, hedgepiggy!" he called, mimicking Tollychook's earnest tones.

Mufus snickered. "Prob'ly not even noticed we're missing!" he said. "Still dawdling about the wood, watching beetles bein' chewed."

Rolling onto his back once more, Bufus gave his mouse tail a wiggle and idly curled and uncurled it while pushing his pink toes into the cool soil.

"Cracked in the head they are," he scoffed. "Waste of time, all that. This is much better."

Mufus spat the stem from his mouth. "All the same," he began, "we really should find a hedgehog of our own. Not to study or anything dull, of course. We could get away with just yanking some bristles out."

"I don't feel like it," his brother moaned.

"If we don't, you know what'll happen. They'll all end up being able to wergle into one before we do—maybe even Gammy. Can't have that, can we?"

Bufus conceded that he had a point. "Mind you," he said, "I haven't seen a hedgehog the whole time we've been here, have you?"

"No," Mufus replied with a scowl. "Come to think of it, I haven't seen anything. No other living thing at all."

His brother yawned. "I reckon the critters hereabouts know when the wergle teaching starts," he said. "So they hide from us. What a fuss over a tiny smudge of fluff."

Mufus rose and peered over the gently swaying grasses. Cocking his head to one side, he waggled his mousy ears but could hear nothing.

"No sound anywhere!" he exclaimed. "Nothin' but the wind a-rustling them bushes down there."

Staring at the dense thickets that grew at the bottom of the sloping heathland, he scratched his head in puzzlement.

"Can't figure it," he muttered.

"P'raps it's always like this out here," Bufus suggested drowsily. "We wouldn't know, would we?"

"Hmm, maybe. Look, I'd best go and see if I can round up one of those prickly cowards. Must all be skulking in them thorn clumps."

Puffing out his chest, he wergled back into his usual self and pulled on his breeches.

"Drive one of them this way," Bufus drawled. "I can't be bothered to go down there."

"I'll scare a whole crowd of 'em out," his brother promised. "You'll be able to pick and choose. Watch out, hedgehogs, Mufus Doolan is coming to get you!"

Cackling like a little demon, he marched through the coarse grasses, down to where the thorns obscured the shores of the Lonely Mere like a bank of dark and jagged fog.

"You can't hide from me," he called in his spookiest voice. "There's no escape. Your dooooom is nigh!"

Cheerily Mufus trotted closer to the dense thickets.

"There'll be bald spots aplenty when I've finished with you!"

The needle-covered branches ahead were rattling and scraping together. Ignorant of the terrible danger, the young werling strolled into their profound shadow with the lightest of hearts.

To the very edge of the thorns he went, then stooped to peer beneath the clattering boughs.

"Come out, come out!" he said, whistling invitingly. "Or I'll come in and kick you out."

The twigs shook even more and Mufus straightened. Something peculiar was happening. Gazing up at the quivering branches, he suddenly realized that the wind was not strong enough to make them bow and bend like that.

"Funny," he murmured. "What's causin' it?"

Mufus began to grow uneasy. It was almost as if the thorns were impatient for him to enter.

Turning back to face the empty stretch of heath, he cupped his hands around his mouth and called, "Hey, Bufus, get down here!"

Only the sighing grasses answered, and then Mufus thought he heard a malevolent, rasping voice hiss behind him.

"Come—come to dark—Snaggart wants."

The werling whisked around.

"Who's that?" he demanded. "Who is it?"

The twigs rattled all the more, and Mufus became afraid. The spiky gloom was suddenly smoldering with menace, and he wanted to run away.

"Bufus!" he shouted in alarm.

Black shapes were moving in those tangled depths, and the werling took a frightened step backward.

At once a pair of pale eyes snapped open in the murk.

Mufus wailed for his brother, and then, to his horror, the thornbush he was standing by shifted and reared upward. From the grass the ogre rose, its buckled legs creaking. In the gnarled head the mouth split open, and twisted arms came swinging round, the fingers of deformed claws jerking and writhing as they reached out to snatch him.

Before Mufus could move another step, the woody talons plucked him off the ground.

"Bufus!" he shrieked. "Bufus, help me! Help!"

The thorn ogres cackled hideously, and into their barbed darkness the werling was dragged.

"Bufus!" Mufus Doolan screamed for the last time, and then his voice was silenced forever.

STILL wearing his mouse shape, Bufus was dozing peacefully.

The whiskers upon his furry face gave an unhappy twitch. Shrill cries had disturbed his slumber, and with a reluctant groan he opened one eye.

"Mufus?" he mumbled dopily. "Where are you?"

Yawning and blinking, the mouse stretched and looked around. The night had become deathly silent once more.

"Mufus?" he said again, a little louder this time.

Bufus sucked his teeth and pouted. Where had his brother gone?

A fuzzy recollection of their last conversation came back to him, and he stared across the heath to where the thornbushes grew. Rubbing the sleep from his eyes, he shouted Mufus's name, but there was still no response.

"What's he doin' down there?" he muttered grumpily. "I'm bored of this and want to go home now."

Sweeping his tail behind him, Bufus wandered over the scrubland, pressing ever closer to the eclipsing mass of thorn and briar.

"Did you find any?" he called. "Did you pull a handful out for me? You'd better or else..."

Drawing near the bushes, Bufus thought he heard thin laughter, and he toddled a little faster toward them.

"What you chucklin' at in there?" he asked. "Mufus, where are you?"

Scampering to the edge of the thicket, the mouse halted. The laughter had stopped and he wavered uncertainly. It wasn't like his brother to play games like this with him.

Thorny branches filled his vision. Bufus did not like the look of those ugly growths. Then something in the corner of his eye made him turn and glance upward.

Bufus Doolan choked back a cry. Above him, impaled upon the spiky twigs, hung Mufus's lifeless body.

The branches rattled, and croaking laughter floated from the shadows.

Howling, Bufus turned tail and ran for his life.

Over the heath the werling pelted, too terrified to even think about wergling back into his proper form. Across that wide, empty desolation he fled, leaping onto the cinder trackway and plunging through the trees beyond.

Not once did he stop. The horrendous image of his brother stuck through with thorns burned like a hot coal in his mind, and squealing hideously, he sped through Hagwood.

Up in the trees around him lanterns were lighted, and anxious faces appeared to see what all the noise was about.

At the base of the wych elm where the Doolans lived, Bufus finally stumbled to a halt and collapsed in the leaf mold.

"'Ware! 'Ware!" he bawled. "Wolves! Owls! Witches! 'Ware! 'Ware!"

Overcome with grief, he buried his face in the dead leaves, wergling back into his usual shape, then wept violently.

The alarm cry had not been used in living memory, and from every home the families came pouring. Down the trees they scrambled, calling to one another in worried voices. What was happening? Some actually believed that a pack of ferocious wolves had invaded, and they refused to leave the safety of the branches. Others thought that there must have been a terrible accident involving one or more of the groups hunting hedgehogs, and parents began to frantically call their children's names. All was panic and confusion, but eventually they gathered around Bufus, who was now being held in his mother's arms, and finally, through his sobs, they heard the ghastly news.

When the horror of his words sank in, the Doolan family wailed and clutched him tightly.

A dismayed hush descended upon the other werlings, and Yoori Mattock stepped forward.

"There will be time for sorrow later," he addressed them. "First we must bring back the child's body."

A great number volunteered to accompany him to the heath, but he ordered that some of them should remain behind.

"The other children must be found," he announced. "This is no night for instruction and study. Find them, fetch them to their homes, and cherish them all the more."

And so, with lanterns and flaming torches in their hands, a host of werlings marched from Hagwood, with Yoori Mattock and Terser Gibble at their head. Fighting their anguish, Bufus Doolan and his parents joined them, for only Bufus could lead them to his brother.

Angered and determined, prepared to fight whatever foes they might encounter, the crowd solemnly crossed the overgrown track and entered the heath.

Down the sloping ground they paraded, with Master Gibble urging them on with encouraging words and warlike cries.

Through the scrubland their tiny lights streaked, tracing a flickering line in that deserted gloom. Then, as the land lifted and became level once more, Bufus gave a shout.

The werlings halted and mustered around him.

"What is it, lad?" Yoori Mattock asked. "Is there aught else we should know?"

Bufus was not listening. He pushed his way through the crowd and stared in disbelief at the heath around him.

"Where are they?" he cried. "Where've they gone?"

The thornbushes had vanished.

Where only a little while ago dense thickets had covered the ground, now only a stretch of stubbly grass separated him from the Lonely Mere in the distance.

"I don't understand!" he yelled. "They were here. I know they were! Mufus was...Mufus was...!"

He could utter no more, and the others looked at him with concern.

Master Gibble drew Yoori Mattock aside.

"An excitable child," the tutor remarked. "He and his brother are prone to pranks. Perhaps this also is one of their little jokes."

Mr. Mattock's whiskery face grew sterner than ever. "I know what the Doolan twins are like," he said. "But just look at the boy. Do you really think he's playacting?"

"I'm sure I don't know," Master Gibble retorted indignantly, his many nostrils all sniffing at once. "Why should my opinion count, after all?"

Yoori rejoined the others. "Before we leave this place," he shouted, "we're going to search it, even if it takes the rest of the night. The poor lad might've fallen into one of the pits. They'll all have to be inspected."

The werlings began at once. Like a slowly bursting firework, the lanterns radiated through the grass and the hunt commenced.

Pursing his lips, Terser Gibble joined the endeavor but with neither enthusiasm nor expectation. He was certain that this was nothing more than an exaggerated mischief, and so, when the grisly discovery was made, he was both astonished and ashamed.

"Here! Here!" one of the searchers called. "I've found… here!"

Lying on the grass was the bloodless body of Mufus Doolan. Punctured with many sharp wounds, it looked as though he had been tossed carelessly aside, a worthless thing to be discarded. It was a contemptible gesture, and no one who looked on that small, broken corpse could staunch their tears.

"What were they doing out here on their own?" Yoori Mattock asked hoarsely. "Who was the leader of their group?"

Master Gibble was dabbing at his nose, making certain that everyone could see how affected he was by this tragedy. "They were in the care of Finnen Lufkin," he answered smartly. "I have no idea why they should come here or why he permitted it."

Mr. Mattock gave instructions for the body to be carried back to Hagwood. "There'll be a meeting of the ruling council tomorrow," he said. "Finnen Lufkin will have a lot of explaining to do."

Trailing wretchedly behind those carrying his brother, Bufus Doolan wiped his streaming eyes and nose and glanced over his shoulder.

The thorns had departed—but where had they gone?

# CHAPTER 11

# The Silent Grove

When they finally crossed the Hagburn and stepped back into their own land, Finnen and the others breathed great glad gulps of the less oppressive air. The horrors they had been through seemed a world away now. This was where they belonged, here in this pleasant corner of Hagwood where the trees were tall and beautiful and all was safe and familiar.

With Gamaliel and the fox cub still in his arms, the Smith gave approving nods at everything he saw.

"A wholesome place," he observed. "Though the shadow of the heartless one has spread far across the wild, no hint of it does Smith perceive here. Long may it remain this way."

It was when they arrived at the Tumpin home that they discovered that evil had already entered in.

Worried that their son's party had not returned when the other groups had been recalled, Figgle and Tidubelle Tumpin were keeping watch in the branches. As the Smith strode over the woodland floor, they saw Gamaliel sitting in the crook of his arm and rushed down the tree as fast as they were able.

"Nuts and pips!" Figgle cried, overjoyed but regarding the Pucca shyly. "Where've you been?"

"We were so worried," Mrs. Tumpin declared, her face unable to decide which smile to wear. "Oh, what a terror this night has been."

The Smith set Gamaliel upon the ground next to them, but when they embraced their son he flinched and his hand flew to his shoulder.

"You're hurt!" they cried, and Figgle stared at the Pucca accusingly, the unseemly squirrel tail flicking angrily behind him.

"Rest is all he requires," the Smith assured them.

Finnen knew what the Tumpins were thinking and was quick to put them right, explaining that it was the Pucca who had saved Gamaliel's life.

"Gave us a lovely licky stew as well," Tollychook added unnecessarily.

Figgle and Tidubelle apologized for leaping to unfair conclusions, but the Smith waved their words aside.

"But where's Kernella?" Gamaliel asked.

Figgle's tail drooped and Tidubelle's smiles faded completely.

"She's gone with the rest," Figgle told them. "To the Silent Grove, to attend the interment. It's Mufus Doolan— he's been killed."

AT THE southernmost tip of the werlings' territory, beyond the hazel tree where they received instruction, the ground dipped into a shallow but wide dingle. Within this broad hollow, many ancient beech trees grew, and beneath their spreading branches, a somber silence lay.

No sound of the surrounding woodland was heard in that hallowed place. Birds refused to nest in the lofty heights, and if they sang nearby their chorus never penetrated the tranquil peace. Even the noise of rustling leaves was muted and reverent.

This was the Silent Grove, a region of gentle calm and serenity, but the werlings hardly ever ventured here and hated doing so. They were not afraid to descend into that quiet dell; no lurking terror kept them at bay. Only the memory of pain and loss compelled them to avoid that spot. The Silent Grove was where those they had loved were finally laid to rest and given back to the forest. This was the werling burial ground.

Finnen's group knew that they must pay their last respects to Mufus. Gamaliel would have gone with them, but his parents forbade it and he was sent straight to bed. The others, however, set off immediately, and still carrying the fox cub (for they could not leave it behind), the Wandering

Smith accompanied them. He was curious about these little people and, for purposes of his own, wished to learn all that he could.

Once they had passed the hazel, they glimpsed the glow of lanterns in the distance, and the nocturnal noises of Hagwood became hushed and still. Only the sound of mournful voices, slowly chanting a melancholy dirge, disturbed the mute shadows.

Beneath the trees the werlings sorrowfully paraded. The profound sadness of the lament blended exquisitely with the stark beauty of the dappling moonlight, and beholding this unfamiliar race at their most private ceremony, the Pucca changed his mind and hung back, removing the helm from his head.

"Smith'll not intrude on such an hour as this," he explained to the others. "The rites of your folk should not be overlooked by any other."

They had come close to the brink of the Silent Grove. The funeral bier had gone down into the night shade of the beeches, and as the Smith watched, the last of the mourners descended after them.

Tollychook glanced at Liffidia and Finnen. "We should go in," he said.

Liffidia agreed, but Finnen resisted. On hearing those grieving voices he felt he had no right to go among them, for he knew he was responsible. The Doolan twins had been in his care, and he had failed them. He could not bring himself to look on the anguish of Mufus's family.

"It wasn't your fault," Liffidia insisted. "You can't blame yourself. We'd all be dead if it wasn't for you. You saved us from Frighty Aggie."

"If it wasn't for me, we wouldn't have gone to her lair in the first place!" Finnen answered. "I should have gone straight to the heath, instead, where Mufus needed me. Everything I've done tonight has been a disaster. He'd still be alive if I hadn't panicked or had been keeping a closer eye on them both."

There was nothing Liffidia could say to ease his conscience. Reaching up, she ruffled the fur behind the fox cub's ears and pledged to return shortly. Then, with Tollychook bumbling alongside, she pattered down the bank.

Gradually the lantern lights wound deeper into the grove, and the Pucca turned to the werling boy at his side.

"Regret and guilt," he began gruffly. "Tie you up tight as the werhag's webs, they will. Smith knows all about them. Don't you reproach yourself over things outside your control. Smith knows where the real blame lies. The foul servants of Rhiannon committed this awful murder. Vile things they are, malignant horrors spawned in the blackness of Her thought. What foulness has She done to raise them? To what new depths has She bent Her evil mind? Her hands are awash with innocent blood."

Finnen found no comfort in his words, and the unlikely pair sat at the edge of the Silent Grove, locked in their own private brooding.

At last the Pucca said, "Never has Smith seen beeches like them yonder. What malady afflicts them so?"

Finnen's long fringe fell across his face as he bent his head, and it was several minutes before he answered.

The trees of the Silent Grove were distorted in shape. Every trunk was covered in unnatural bulges and crusty swellings. Up into the high, sturdy boughs the tumorous growths reached. Some were only slight lumps or budding nodules, but there were many large, cragged carbuncles that barreled and stretched the bagging bark.

"They're not diseased," Finnen revealed. "It's us, those are our grave markers."

Hurrying in the wake of the trailing procession, Tollychook and Liffidia tagged themselves onto the end of the mourners. Presently they halted by one of the gibbous beeches, and the werlings congregated around it, encircling the bumpy trunk.

Arms outstretched, Master Gibble stepped forward and in a loud, imploring voice called, "Blessed beech. Mother of the Forest you are! Here we have brought to you one of your sons. Receive and keep him, we beg."

The stretcher that carried Mufus's corpse was laid on the ground, and the Doolan family stroked and kissed him one final time. Then slender ropes were tied to each of the bier's four corners, and Master Gibble clambered up the tree, composed and dignified.

High he climbed, to where the trunk divided, then higher still—until he reached a place where the lumps were only faint blisters.

Two stout and strong werlings, bearing the four ropes, followed him and ascended even higher, throwing the lines over sturdy branches above their heads. When they were in position, Master Gibble gave the sign and they began to heave on the cables.

Below them, the Doolans wept as their dead son was lifted off the ground, and Bufus sprang forward, his grief raging.

"I won't let him go!" he shrieked, clutching at the stretcher. "Don't take him away! Don't!"

His father pulled him clear, and the bier was hoisted out of reach.

"MUFUS!" his brother howled.

Perched upon the bough, the Wergle Master spread his tapering fingers over the moderate undulations of the beech tree and pressed his lips to the bark. Then in a low, worshipful voice he recited:

> *"Beech, beech, blessed beech.*
> *Within your timbers our long past slumbers.*
> *Great is that list of those we have missed,*
> *But open and keep another who sleeps.*
> *Take him now—away from reach."*

The mourners at the base of the tree joined their hands and closed their eyes. Almost imperceptibly they began to hum—one long, protracted note.

The droning accord grew steadily louder, and in response, the branches of the beech tree shivered and swayed. The mystery of the werling interment was commencing, and the age-old miracle occurred anew.

From the bottom-most roots, a slow tremor rippled up the trunk, sluggishly flowing up into the branches in a spiraling wave, surging just below the knobbed surface.

Upon the quivering branches, tiny buds burst forth, blossoming with purple, tassel-like flowers that danced and trembled. Their rustling was like a whispering music that made a fragile harmony with the humming of the werlings. In the heart of every bloom a bright dew burned with a golden light, and the welling radiance streamed through the grove, dispelling the midnight gloom.

Rich rays of summer shone over the branches, and the bark beneath Master Gibble's palms rolled and pulsed. Then, with his fingernail, he drew a line along the soft and mushing rind.

Into the yielding wood the mark sank, becoming a furrow that deepened into a crack, which became a cleft—creeping wider and wider apart until a great hole had opened up in that mighty bough. A delicate fragrance of sweet musty decay arose from the strange chasm, and the tutor's nostrils quivered.

"Raise him," he called to the rope handlers.

Over that newly gaping gulf, the stretcher was heaved into position, and Master Gibble guided its course with his spindly fingers.

"Blessed beech!" he called aloud. "You are the book in which our forebears are recorded. Closely do you keep their names, from first to last. Accept, then, another, to guard and protect him in the mansion of the dead. Here is Mufus Doolan, outside our care now. Thus, unto yours do we commend him."

The ropes that tethered the stretcher by Mufus's feet were lowered gently, and the Doolan boy's body slid down into the dark, waiting grave.

Slowly the edges of the gap pushed inward, and the bark closed together, sealing Mufus within for as long as the tree should endure.

Far below, his brother screwed up his face and dug his fists into his eyes.

The scintillating light grew dim, and the mysterious

blossoms fell from the branches, dropping to the floor with the sound of soft rain. Dun shadows returned, the resonant humming faded to silence, and the tree ceased its trembling.

"It is done," Master Gibble proclaimed. "Let us remember him and the others we have been parted from."

The ceremony was over, and the mourners began to disperse through the grove, pausing at certain trees. Some of the werlings caressed the rugged projections, while others watered the ground with tears.

Outside, but not removed from this despair, the Smith stroked his beard and his eyes glinted.

"A strange folk you are," he said in wonderment.

"It's always been this way," Finnen told him. "There's nothing strange about it. We all know where our final resting place will be. The Lufkin tree is over there. We go to the beeches; they are the wardens of our dead."

"But the growths, why are they so uneven in size?"

"The lumps grow where we are placed. The really big bumps show where a Grand Wergle Master is interred. It has to do with how strong the wergling gift was in whoever lies there. It affects the wood somehow."

"The transforming skill must run mighty in your family," the Pucca observed. "Yon Lufkin tree seems fair to rupturing."

Finnen averted his eyes.

At that moment the fox cub began to squirm in the Pucca's arms, for Liffidia was returning. Kernella Tumpin was with her. Tollychook had found his parents among the crowd and had already begun the journey back with them.

"Ooh, Finnen!" Gamaliel's sister cried, giving the outlandish and tall Smith a wide berth. "I was so worried about you. You must tell me everything. There's been such a lot going on that if I don't go pop with my nerves it'll be an amazement. Why did the Doolans go to the heath on their own? Everyone wants to know. What have you done to your arm; why's it in a sling?"

Before the boy could answer, the Pucca placed the helm back on his head and declared that it was time he departed.

"The night grows old," he said. "Smith has the great matter to attend to. By morning the land may be cleansed, and there will be no more senseless slaughter of children."

Finnen bade him farewell and wished him luck.

"Will you come back?" he asked.

The Pucca smiled grimly. "Of that there's no doubt; Smith'll have to."

Finnen wondered if there was more to those words than he could guess, for the Pucca had looked at him strangely.

But there was no time to ponder on hidden meanings for with a bow the Smith took his leave. When he had taken the fox cub to Liffidia's home, he would begin the journey back to his encampment.

Kernella and Finnen were alone.

"I didn't like the look of that great giant," she snorted. "Who was he? Some grubby beggar of the big folk, I shouldn't wonder. What you taking up with the likes of him for?"

Finnen sighed. He was tired and had been through too much already without having to face the ordeal of Kernella Tumpin's interrogation.

"If you want to know, you'll have to wait till the morning, like the rest of them," he said bluntly. "I'd like to be on my own now. I want to go over to the Lufkin tree."

His words could have been chosen with greater care and tact, for Kernella took both the cue and offense. Pressing her lips together, she flounced away.

The Silent Grove was deserted. The mourners had returned to their homes. All was quiet and hushed once again. The venerable calm of the beech trees had returned and would not be disturbed again until the passing of another werling.

Finnen glanced cautiously around him, then stepped down into the tranquil dingle. Purposefully he strode toward the tree that housed the deceased members of the Lufkin family, and standing in its shadow, he lifted his face. It was wrung with remorse and shame.

"Forgive me," he whispered.

Very slowly, because of the injury to his arm, he began to climb. Up over the beech's many rumpled bulges he went, scaling those bunioned bellies while quoting the names of his ancestors.

"Channin Luffud, Meldit Luffud—the Grand Wergle Master, Hootil Luffud, Fashana Lufkin—the elder, Sifkin Lufkin, Fashana Lufkin—the adept, Gremiggan Lufkin, Porfi Lufkin—the Great Adept, Wirfol Lufkin—Great Grand Wergle Master..."

It was a prodigious, honorable list, and when he reached a cleft in the trunk, Finnen's ascent ceased.

Two immense limbs covered with vast swellings mounted the night on either side, and turning to face a particularly large and warty protuberance, the boy bowed in respect.

"Mahfti Lufkin—Supreme Wergle Master, one of the most gifted of our race, second only to Agnilla Hellekin. Pardon this wretch, your humble descendant. I was not blessed with your skill."

Unclasping the leather bag at his belt, the very one that Frighty Aggie had pored over, Finnen took out a tiny whittling knife. A shudder ran through his body and his face contorted with self-loathing, but there was no going back.

"You can't stop now," he told himself. "You ought never to have begun—oh, if only I'd never set foot here."

The hand that held the knife was trembling.

"Do it quick!" Finnen urged. "Then you can get away. Quickly now!"

Raising the blade close to the lumpy growth that marked the resting place of his exalted forebear, he closed his eyes in disgust and started shaving the bark away.

In the small bag, he collected the parings.

Many years ago, Agnilla Hellekin had reaped a similar harvest. By chewing slivers of wood garnered from the grave markers of past Wergle Masters, she had greatly increased her already formidable powers. Finnen had heard the tale from his grandmother, and when he failed at his first wergling attempt, he had foolishly dared to do the same. Now he despised himself for it.

"What will become of you?" he mumbled, repulsed by his own actions. "A cheat and a liar you were, and a coward—for if you had any courage you would never have done this revolting thing. Now someone has lost his life because of you. Finnen Lufkin, you're a murderer as well."

Weeping, he crawled down the beech tree and stumbled home.

At the edge of the Silent Grove, a gangly figure stepped from the shadows where it had been hiding, and a spiteful sneer crept over its long-nosed face.

"My successor, indeed!" Terser Gibble spat.

# Chapter 12
# The Death of Gofannon

Through the wild forest the Pucca hurried. The tyrannic rule of the High Lady Rhiannon would end that very night.

"To Her own carrion birds Smith'll feed Her sequestered heart," he vowed. "Scatter the last beakful to the four winds and in Her halls She'll drop stone dead. Aye, then we'll do what's right. A gentler ruler will take up the crown; Smith'll see to that."

Approaching his encampment, the Pucca went straight to his handcart and drew out a gleaming sword. The tempered blade rang musically, but even before the note faded, the Smith hissed under his breath and the whiskers of his beard began to tingle. Something was horribly wrong.

"The night is thick with watchful eyes," he whispered, backing away warily. "The servants of the enemy are here."

Whirling around, he dashed back the way he had come, lunging desperately through the trees with the sword sweeping before him. But it was too late; he had entered the trap and now it snapped shut about him.

A ferocious clamor suddenly broke out, and the darkness was filled with raucous yells. From the encircling trees evil shapes with small shining eyes came springing, and crashing into the Pucca's path to prevent his escape were three enormous thorn ogres.

The Smith skidded to a halt before their fearsome, cackling faces and looked wildly behind him.

It seemed as if the whole forest teemed and heaved with those foul creatures. From every shadow the horrors charged. The full strength of Rhiannon's malevolent army had descended from the cold hills where She had bred them, and their infernal shrieks trumpeted in the Pucca's ears. Into the little clearing of his encampment they swarmed, overturning his cart and baying for death. Devils of thorn and hate they were—snarling, screeching fiends—and over all their heads the barn owl circled, calling the commands of their pitiless mistress.

"Take him!" it hooted. "Seize the hated thief!"

There were too many for the Smith to overcome. Rank upon rank of the savage brutes rampaged toward him, and all hope died. Yet he would not be captured without dispatching as many of his foes as he was able.

"Thimbleglaive!" he cried. "Fly and fight. Let your steel cut the night."

From his belt the enchanted knife bolted, instantly hurling itself at the raging enemy.

Glittering like a cold splinter of moonlight, it plunged and stabbed. Grasping claws were sliced apart, eyes burning with malice were rapidly extinguished, and shrieking gullets were razored. Bellowing, the ogres fell before the blade's slashing volleys, but for every slain monster there were countless others to take its place.

While his knife dealt darting death, the Smith grasped the hilt of his sword and swung it into the woody necks of the fiends that leaped in front of him.

"For Angirrion!" he roared, splitting a repulsive spiny-crowned head in two. "For Gromer! Gwyddno! Diarmund and Cormac!"

Three more ogres tumbled under the sword's lethal blows, and the Smith sprang onto the hill of their bodies to wield even greater threat and peril to those who surged around him.

"For Bodach and Hafgan and Launfal!" he thundered. "For all of my kindred whose blood She shed unjustly!"

Like one possessed he battled, striving with every raging breath against that berserking horde, and many screeched their last before his fury. But their number was overwhelming, and soon his strokes began to lose their strength and go astray. Long claws darted in and raked his skin. Others snatched at his hair and beard while the helm was knocked from his head.

Then, clambering over the mound of its fallen comrades, the greatest of those nightmares came grinning.

"Naggatash—Naggatash!" the other ogres chanted.

Trampling the dead beneath its huge clubbed feet, the chieftain of the thorn ogres came. Over the humps of its wide back the thorny branches grew stout and strong, and its hide was like the armored bark of the firstborn, storm-seasoned trees. A strip of braided twigs banded its projecting forehead, displaying its high rank, and the eyes that glared at the beleaguered Smith were dark windows into its hellish, malignant mind.

"Naggatash!" came the spurring calls. "Naggatash! Naggatash!"

Bracing himself for another assault, the Smith lunged and the sword sang.

Up onto its trunklike legs Naggatash reared, and a horrendous bawling shriek rumbled in its throat.

Down sliced the sword and the Smith pushed all his flagging strength into the attack.

A deafening discord penetrated the entire breadth of Hagwood as the Pucca's steel clashed violently against the ogre's iron-hard shoulder. There was a dazzling flash of sparks and the blade bit into the apparition's hide. But the blow had been too fierce, and the thorny armor of Naggatash was bound about with troll witch spells.

A juddering, jolting vibration traveled the length of the blade. The hilt was ripped from the Smith's hands as, suddenly, the sword shattered as though made of glass.

With the broken tip still lodged in its shoulder, Naggatash laughed horribly, and the surrounding host shrieked their foul glee.

Robbed of his sword, the defenseless Pucca saw the huge chieftain prowl toward him, and in the depths of those eyes he saw himself reflected, a puny, helpless figure staring at the advance of his own death.

"Hold him!" the owl demanded from above.

The ogre's grin leered even wider, and then it pounced.

Only one chance remained, and the Smith cried out at the top of his voice.

"Thimbleglaive!"

Still weaving a flickering net of deadly light in the army's midst, the enchanted knife came streaking through the air. Before the terrible chieftain's claws could close about its master, the dagger plummeted straight into the furrows between the monster's eyes.

A guttural gasp escaped Naggatash's jaws, and the massive legs crumpled beneath its great bulk. Down it smashed, and the malice behind those dark eyes perished.

It was the Pucca's last victory.

The besieging ogres screeched with rage at the loss of their chieftain and rushed to avenge him.

"Thimbleglaive!" the Smith called.

But the knife was embedded deep in the head of Naggatash. Jerking and quivering, it struggled to free itself, but it was clamped fast and firm in that dense skull, and there it remained. The trembling stopped and the magic failed.

The Pucca was powerless and vulnerable, and the ogres flung themselves upon him.

Sharp grasping talons tore at him, barbed hooks caught

his skin, woody stems cracked against his head, and he was captured.

Battered and bleeding, the Smith was hurled into the air then dashed to the ground close to his overturned handcart, where the frenzied hatred of the enemy overran him.

"Enough!" the barn owl screeched. "He must not be slain—not yet."

Snarling, the ogres fell back, and the bird alighted upon one of the cart's buckled wheels.

The gold of its eyes shone with gloating triumph, and it regarded the Smith's beaten face without mercy.

"Little thief," the owl spoke with arch contempt. "What of thy grand design now? Still my mistress lives, but thy tale hath nearly ended."

Striped and crossed with bright scarlet cuts, the Smith returned the bird's condemning stare.

"Go back to the hag who hatched you!" he spat.

The owl chuckled wickedly. "Still thy manners are wanting," it said. "Yet again I charge thee to yield that which thou didst steal. Return that precious property unto its rightful owner."

It was the Pucca's turn to laugh: a bleak, piteous sound in that awful place. "Little good would it do Her!" he scorned. "Nay, only Smith could put that thing to any use. You will never learn its whereabouts from his lips."

"Shall I not?" the owl retorted. "Many are the devices in the dark dungeons of the cold hills, diverse instruments to gouge and draw. By the morrow the torture masters will have picked the lock of thy insolent tongue."

Spreading its wings, the barn owl instructed the ogres to bear the Smith away.

Once again powerful claws seized his limbs, and he was hoisted roughly above their repugnant heads.

Racked with fatigue and weakened by the stinging pain of his wounds, the Pucca was filled with dread at the horrific ordeal that awaited him. In this, the messenger of Rhiannon spoke the truth. Under torment he might indeed divulge where the casket containing the High Lady's heart was hidden, and he cursed himself.

"Fires take him!" he ranted. "See where his white liver has brought him! Why did he not destroy the thing those many years ago?"

His captors cackled to hear him wailing, and they tightened their grip on his arms and legs, squeezing until the sinews parted to make him yelp some more.

Onto the mound of slaughtered ogres, Snaggart the rat-like creature went bounding to get a better view as they carried him by. Reveling in the Pucca's distress, it capered madly, clapping its hands and gibbering.

"Pinch—punch!" it yapped. "More squeals—more squeals—Snaggart like—Snaggart like! Stick it—poke it!"

As it was prancing, the ogre's squint eyes fell upon the Smith's dagger, still lodged firmly in Naggatash's skull. It licked its lips covetously.

"Snaggart want!" it barked.

Grasping the handle, the ogre tugged, but it would not budge. Flapping with frustration, it planted one foot squarely on the dead chieftain's brow, then took hold once more and heaved.

"Snaggart have!" it growled, clenching its jaws. "Snaggart pull!"

The dagger twisted in the wound, and a trickle of Naggatash's blood oozed out.

"Snaggart take!" came the straining shout.

With that the blade sprang from the monster's skull, and Snaggart somersaulted backward.

At once he scurried back to the top of the heap, flourishing the dripping blade as he danced a clumsy jig.

"Mine—mine!" he shrieked, vastly pleased with himself.

Past the mound where Snaggart cavorted, the ogres carried the Wandering Smith. The imp's crowing cries rose above all other noises, and the Pucca craned his head to look on that frolicking creature.

A glint of green burned in the Smith's eyes. Perhaps there was a chance, after all. He would keep his secret and cheat them still.

The embers of hope burst into new flame within him, and a grim smile parted his beard.

"Thimbleglaive," he murmured.

Flying above him, the owl suddenly saw what Snaggart was brandishing and espied the Pucca staring at it intently.

"Cover his mouth!" the bird squawked in alarm. "Stifle his words!"

But it was already too late.

"Trusty knife, trusty knife," the Pucca had muttered. "Fly to me and take my life."

From Snaggart's unsuspecting claws the dagger flew. Up it soared, scribing a bright, clear, and graceful line in the air—then down it came.

A welcoming laugh was on the Smith's lips, and the enchanted knife dived swiftly into his breast.

"Fools!" the owl screeched.

Swooping from above, the bird plucked at the dagger with its feet, but there was nothing it could do; the Pucca was dying.

"Where is the casket?" it shrieked, beating its wings in his face. "Where? Answer! Answer!"

"Not this day or any other, Master Flat Face," came the Smith's failing voice.

"Foul felon!" the owl screamed, quaking with impotent wrath. "Thou wilt tell me! Thou wilt! Rhiannon demands it!"

Abruptly the bird stilled its fury, and its golden eyes stared off into the gloom.

A terrified hush descended, and the thorn ogres fell on their faces, groveling in the dirt.

"Witchmother!" they jabbered with awe.

"My Lady!" the owl exclaimed.

The Smith rolled his eyes sideways, and a gently mocking smile drifted across his features. His last glimpse of the living world was of the night-clad trees nearby, where a slender figure stepped from the gloom, wrapped in a mantle of shimmering shadow.

Achingly beautiful, the Lady Rhiannon was like a pinnacle of graven ice. Framed by the pall of her raven hair, the bleached white face was hard and cold, devoid of any softness and purged of tender feeling.

No light sparkled in her large, loveless eyes, and she regarded the Pucca with chill disdain.

"He is dead?" her leaden voice asked.

"Dying, Majesty," the owl announced. "Soon to expire."

The cloak furling about her, she remained in the shrouding dark—dispassionate and remote.

"Did he speak?"

Before the bird could answer, a sighing breath came from the Pucca's lips.

"Murdering witch," he gasped. "Well met after...after all the parting years."

"Gofannon." The High Lady addressed him by his true name, and the edge in her voice was as keen and deadly as whetted steel. "Ignoble and base has your wastrel life been outside our court. Redeem yourself in these parting moments. Atone and repent your arch treason."

A low chuckle rattled in the Pucca's throat. "Ne'er shall you be safe, Rhiannon Rigantona," he warned in a hoarse whisper. "The box you do not and sh-shall never have. Your own ending approaches. With the far sight of those close to death, Smith sees it truly. A fire he has kindled, and in its heat your doom is ready wrought. Your vile works will crumble and you will burn in ruin. Smith goes with a glad heart, for he has denied you yours..."

The smile remained traced upon his lips, but the Wandering Smith spoke no more.

"We are displeased, our Provost," the Lady Rhiannon said to the owl. "We have not bided his long absence to be hindered here at the last. Tear his paltry cart to pieces and examine his peasant belongings. If you find naught there then scour every inch of this squalid woodland. The casket must be found!"

The owl bowed before her, and with a final, maleficent look at the Pucca's body, the High Lady moved back into the dark. There was a flurry of fallen leaves and a chill wind blew through the forest.

"What of the thief? Mistress?" the bird inquired.

Her voice came floating from the invisible, and it was frozen with contempt.

"Let our pets search him—to his very marrows."

# CHAPTER 13
# The Trial
# of Finnen Lufkin

The first light of morning was gray and drear. In a deep burrow, excavated beneath the roots of a wild apple tree that was too old and hoary to bear any fruit, the presiding council of the werlings met.

It was a large, dome-shaped chamber, lit by seven lanterns suspended from the earthen, root-knotted ceiling. Old dusty banners bearing the badges of the most important families wafted gently in the musty air, and behind a long, crescent-curved table, the six council members settled themselves in their seats. Their faces were grave and solemn.

Yoori Mattock was present, as well as Terser Gibble. Only the worthiest folk had a place in that assembly. Twice a season they gathered together to debate the well-being and circumstances of their kind. The matters they discussed were usually minor affairs: repairs to the hazel platform, disputes over dwellings, which tree to colonize next, and quibbles on aspects of wergling law such as whether certain persons ought to be allowed to retain spare appendages like squirrel tails.

Occasionally the more boisterous elements of their society gave cause for a little concern, but they were certainly not disruptive enough to warrant punishment. There was practically no trouble from outside their borders, and because of their shape-changing talents, there were few other creatures who were even aware of them. Serious problems hardly ever arose.

The previous night had changed all that.

Upon a low bench against the wall, the Doolan family sat. Their faces were pale and haggard, testaments to their grief, but Bufus looked the worst of all.

Sullen and silent, he stared at the floor, waiting to be called to the table to give his account of what had occurred, but all that he wanted was to have his brother back.

Across the chamber Finnen, Liffidia, and Tollychook sat upon another bench. It had been decided that Gamaliel's testimony could wait until later in the day because of the injury to his shoulder—that and the fact that his mother stubbornly refused to wake him at that early hour.

Taking up a small ceremonial hammer, a wrinkled werling called Diffi Maffin, the great-aunt of Stookie Maffin, tapped the table and pronounced the meeting open. Shuffling a sheaf of blank papers and cutting a new quill, Niffer Muglitt, the council recorder, hoped he had enough ink, and the proceedings began.

"Great is the sadness that hangs over our land this day," Yoori Mattock stated. "A child has been killed while out on the important business of instruction. Here, in the cold reason of morning we must discover if the untimely death of Mufus Doolan could have been prevented and just how that tragedy occurred. The exact circumstances must be investigated and established so that we may learn and no such incident will ever befall us again."

Mr. Muglitt's pen ceased its scratching, and Irvinn Goilok, an aged fellow who had an irritating habit of fiddling with his ears, cleared his throat.

"Let the first witness approach the council," he called, with his forefinger already probing his left lug hole. "Liffidia Nefyn, step forward."

Liffidia obeyed and gave a true account of how the Doolans had disappeared and everything that happened afterward.

The expressions of the council members dissolved from portraits of dignified sobriety into caricatured masks of shock and amazement. Finally, when they heard how Finnen had fought Frighty Aggie, one of the elders, Benwin Ortle, slapped the table to interrupt her.

"Stop, girl!" he demanded. "What ludicrous nonsense is this? How dare you mock us with your fanciful lies!"

"Stick to the truth," Yoori advised sternly.

Liffidia glared at them. "I'm not lying!" she retorted. "That's just what happened. How can you not believe me?"

The six councillors spoke among themselves, and Terser Gibble uttered something in a whisper.

Mr. Mattock raised his white, whiskery eyebrows in surprise at whatever the tutor had told him and addressed Liffidia again. "Is it true," he began, "that you find the furbishment of wergle pouches to be cruel, and that you had never believed in Frighty Aggie before you began instruction? Did you not, in fact, wish to wergle into an insect?"

"Yes," she admitted. "But I don't see what that has to—"

"Stand down," Irvinn told her, removing the finger from his ear and wagging its wax-coated tip at her. "You're an unreliable witness. Tollychook Umbelnapper, come forth."

Flushed and angry, Liffidia returned to her seat, and Tollychook bashfully went to stand in her place.

"Tell us," Mr. Mattock began. "Why did you cross the Hagburn and leave Mufus and Bufus behind?"

Tollychook stared shyly at the floor and fidgeted with his hands. That morning he had finally removed the handkerchief from around his nose, but the mouse's teeth marks were still clearly visible. "It were them Doolans' fault," he burbled. "Not meanin' no disrespect to him what's gone, you understand."

"How were they to blame?" Benwin Ortle asked.

"Cos they scarpered and left us."

"They went into the wild forest, and you followed them, is that it?"

"Yes—or leastways, no. They didn't akshully go that way, but Finnen thought they had."

Diffi Maffin frowned, and the many lines of her face crinkled and spread over her features like ripples expanding across a pool.

"And is that where you met the outsider?" she asked. "One of the big folk—a wild ruffian from all appearances. Just the sort of villain we have always kept ourselves hidden from. Why did you consort with him and bring him to the interment?"

Tollychook sniffed unhappily. "He saved us," he said.

"Liffidia Nefyn has told us that it was Finnen who saved you. The story changes at every turn."

"Oh, he did!" Tollychook cried. "Them both did. Then Old Smith, he give us a root stew. Nice, it were."

The councillors blinked at him, and Mr. Muglitt's quill snapped, splattering the paper with ink.

"Are we to understand," Yoori Mattock said, incredulous and astonished, "that while Mufus Doolan was being murdered, you were not even searching for him but were enjoying a hearty supper?"

Tollychook's face crumpled and he began to cry.

"Sit down," Yoori commanded.

Next it was the turn of Bufus Doolan, and the boy shambled to the desk, his eyes raw and red.

The council regarded him kindly, and Niffer hastily cut another quill.

"In your own time," Mr. Mattock prompted in a soft, sympathetic voice. "Why did you go to the heath?"

Bufus cast a sidelong glance at Finnen and the others before speaking.

"Mufus...Mufus and me," he began haltingly, "we just went. I know we shouldn't have but...we couldn't help it."

"Did you see what happened to your brother? Who or what committed this fiendish crime?"

Bufus shook his head wretchedly.

"Why did you not tell anyone where you and Mufus were headed?" Irvinn asked.

The boy lifted his tearstained face and in an angry voice replied, "We did! We told 'em right enough. Lufkin knew we wanted to go to the heath; we'd said so. He should have come fetched us, but he didn't. He was supposed to. We didn't know no better!"

The eyes of the councillors fell upon Finnen Lufkin, and Bufus's father spluttered, "It's his fault! His fault my son's dead!"

Mr. Doolan sprang to his feet and started lurching across the chamber with his fists clenched, but his wife pleaded with him and grabbed at his arm. Leaping from her seat, Liffidia yelled in her friend's defense and Tollychook gabbled in dismay. The ceremonial hammer rapped a brisk tattoo upon the table as Diffi Maffin called for order to be restored. Throughout this uproar Finnen remained silent and still, avoiding all their glances.

When a brittle calm had settled, Irvinn Goilok called, "Finnen Lufkin, step up."

The hero of the werling children rose, and with his arm still in a sling, he stood before them.

Lacing his spindly fingers together, Terser Gibble eyed him coldly.

"Is it true?" Benwin Ortle asked. "Did the Doolan twins tell you they wanted to go to the heath?"

"They did," came his plain answer.

Mr. Doolan rumbled threateningly and Liffidia called out, "But they wanted to see the holly fence as well! We all thought that's where they were headed, not just Finnen."

"One more outburst from you, young Nefyn," Mr. Goilok snapped, "and you will be told to leave."

Yoori Mattock took up the questioning.

"Do you also admit that you purposely wasted precious time with an unknown vagrant?"

Finnen stared Mr. Mattock straight in the eye. "We weren't wasting time!" he said impatiently. "Last night the Wandering Smith told us of the High Lady in the Hollow Hill..."

"What ails the lad?" Mistress Maffin exclaimed. "We are not here to discuss such things. What have they to do with us?"

"Everything!" Finnen replied, his temper simmering. "There's something big going on out there. It was the servants of the Lady Rhiannon who killed Mufus. The Smith is the only one who can save us. If he fails, then there'll be more murders and nowhere will be safe. We ought to be out there helping him."

The council members covered their ears.

"Silence!" Yoori shouted. "We will hear no more. It is now plain to see where the impressionable minds in your charge learn their prattling falsehoods. How dare you utter such wicked lies about the royal folk of the Hill! What mania is in you, lad? I had heard that you were one to be trusted and had much respect. I cannot guess how you acquired such a reputation, for you are nothing but an idler and a lying coward. Is it any wonder the Doolan children desired their own company, away from you?"

Mr. Mattock turned to Terser Gibble, who was still considering Finnen down his long nose, the nostrils of which were slowly dilating and shrinking in time to the pulse of his thoughts.

"Master Gibble," Yoori entreated, "I look to you for guidance in this matter. It is evident that the blame of this tragedy lies with the Lufkin lad, but it is a muddy affair, made none the clearer for the wilful deceits told by himself and his companions. What course shall we take?"

Finnen could not believe them. "Why aren't you listening?" he cried. "If something isn't done, if the High Lady isn't got rid of—then nothing will ever be the same again. Wergling won't keep us safe from the poison-tipped arrows of her soldiers. Her power is spreading!"

"What has happened to our young folk?" Irvinn Goilok asked in sorry bemusement.

The nostrils in Terser Gibble's nose winked shut as he took a sharp breath and left his seat.

"As for the Nefyn girl," the tutor remarked, speaking aloud for the first time during the whole of the meeting, "she suffers from lack of discipline and needs to feel the rod against her back. A sound thrashing never hurt anybody. That will curb her pert impudence and ensure her loyalty does not get misplaced again. Tollychook Umbelnapper, however, is too clod-stupid to know any better and has merely fallen in with the wrong company."

Striding around the table, Master Gibble licked his mottled teeth and considered Finnen with the utmost distaste.

"For you see," he said, wearing a face of vinegar, "there has flourished in our midst a most hideous criminal, an assassin of all that we cherish and hold dear. I speak, of course, of the nauseating worm that is Finnen Lufkin!"

Master Gibble revolved on his heel, then pointed an accusing finger at the boy, and his beady eyes flashed with enmity.

"There really isn't time for this," Finnen said, ripping the sling away and throwing both hands in the air. "Some of us should go back into the forest and see if the Smith is still there. If he's managed to destroy Her then we can go on wergling into mice and frogs till we fall over, but if he hasn't then we have to know so we can prepare ourselves!"

"Never have I known such perfidy!" Terser Gibble ranted, shouting the boy into silence. "A viper in our bosom, that's what he is! A most heinous and obdurate poltroon, a mucid abscess that must be cut from our bodies, and I, Terser Gibble, shall denounce and expose this impenitent, obscene outrage to you all! Behold the vile dissembler; see what foulness he has been perpetrating!"

The tutor's hands snatched a small leather bag from Finnen's belt and, with a toss of his head, emptied the contents onto the floor.

Out fell the chippings Finnen had taken from the Silent Grove, and uttering a dismal groan, the boy closed his eyes. His horrible secret was out.


GAMALIEL Tumpin awoke at noon. His dreams had been dark and troubled, but the sleep had refreshed him, and he now felt ready for the day.

Stretching in his untidy bed of moss and straw, he whimpered at the pain in his shoulder and peeped under the fresh bandage his mother had placed there.

"I'll have a whopping scar," he observed, pulling a face. "Still, the Smith knew what he was doing. Just a dull ache now."

Gazing round his messy bedchamber, he smiled at the sight of his crowded collections, but the pleasure fell instantly from his face when he remembered that Mufus Doolan was dead.

The Doolans always had teased him, and Gamaliel often had wished that they would go away, but never had he wished for anything like this to happen to either of them. A mild, irrational guilt washed over him, and he reenacted the previous night in his mind. At the time it had all flashed by so quickly, and after the encounter with Frighty Aggie he hadn't even given them a second thought.

But there were other things to think about. Everything the Smith had told them was still bright and terrible in his memory, and he looked around for his clothes so that he could go and discuss it with the others.

In just a few minutes he was hopping up the passage, pulling his shoes on, when he heard a sound that made him falter and stumble.

It was coming from Kernella's room. She was crying.

Puzzled, for he did not realize that his sister had been especially fond of Mufus Doolan, he ventured to her doorway and peeped inside.

Kernella Tumpin's chamber was neat and spartan. The moss of her bed was mingled with sweetly scented leaves and the dried petals of last autumn's flowers, and the crackly mixture was plumped and pushed into the corner every morning. Two large baskets contained her neatly folded clothes, and consigned to the orderly shelves were the neglected rag dolls and trinkets of her childish past.

With her face in her hands, she sat on a stool, weeping and sniveling. She did not hear her brother enter until he announced his presence by coughing.

Normally Kernella would have scolded him for invading her room, and Gamaliel prepared himself for a verbal bashing, but the girl merely lifted her head and sobbed all the more.

Gamaliel had never seen her so upset. His first anxious thought was that something awful had happened to their parents during the night.

"It's Finnen!" Kernella wailed, dispelling his instinctive fears. "Oh...it's too...oh!"

"What about him?" her brother demanded. "Is he all right?"

Kernella shook her head and blew her nose. "Nooo," she whined. "He lied to me. He lied to everyone!"

Gamaliel knelt before her. "Why? What's gone on?"

"He was cheatin' the whole time!" she cried. "It's so awful an' nasty, what he done. It makes me sick! I hate him—I hate him!"

"Kernella!" Gamaliel exclaimed. "You're not making sense. What did he do?"

The girl sobbed a little more, then took heaving breaths. "He weren't no better at wergling than the rest of us," she eventually declared, mopping her eyes. "Weren't cleverer or gifted at all. He was going to the Silent Grove and stealing slivers of wood from the trees to increase his wergle powers. Oh, Gamaliel, he were chewin' and eatin' them. It's so disgusting—how could he?"

Gamaliel drew back, aghast.

"That's revolting," he murmured. "It can't be true. Finnen wouldn't do anything like that."

Wringing her hands, Kernella began crying all over again.

"But he did!" she blubbed. "Master Gibble saw him. There was a meetin' of the council this mornin', and he emptied Finnen's bag on the floor. It were full of shavings and splinters. He's been deceivin' everyone and has made a complete fool out of me."

Gamaliel drew himself up; he did not know what to do or how to feel. Finnen's crime appalled him, but the longer he thought about it the more he understood the reason. If anyone knew about the pressures of wergling instruction, Gamaliel did. Had he known about the powers that the wood of the Silent Grove possessed, would he have resisted the temptation? He was not certain.

"You don't hate Finnen really," he told his sister. "He couldn't help himself, and once he started he wasn't able to stop. No one would let him alone. He never pushed himself forward or said he was the best. We did that; we were always doing it. He never had a chance."

Kernella sniffed. "Don't matter if I hate him or not," she mumbled. "Too late now."

"What does that mean?"

"The council," she said, her words tumbling out. "When they heard what he'd done, they were so horrified that they sentenced him to exile. Finnen's been banished— sent over the Hagburn. He were only allowed to say good- bye to his nan, then he had to go. Mother and Father are with her now, poor old thing. Oh, it was hideous, Gamaliel.

Word had got out about what he'd done and how he was to blame for Mufus's death as well. There was a crowd. Some folk threw stones. I'll never forget the look on his face. It was so hurt, so unhappy, and that's the last I ever saw of him. I'll never see Finnen Lufkin again!"

In a turmoil, Gamaliel could hardly believe what she was saying. "Why didn't you wake me?" he asked. "Why didn't you tell me? I should have been there. I could have done something."

"It was over so quick," his sister explained wretchedly. "If I'd have come up here, I'd have missed his going as well."

Gamaliel's eyes were stinging with the threat of his own tears. "That's not fair," he muttered. "Just not fair. The council didn't have to do that. It's mean and cruel!"

The injustice of the elders' decision stunned him, but swiftly his simmering resentment boiled into anger, and Gamaliel Tumpin thumped the wall in frustration.

"I won't have it!" he shouted. "Finnen saved all our lives last night. I don't care what else he's done, I'm not letting him go off like that without so much as a word of thanks."

Kernella stared at him in surprise. That didn't sound like her useless little brother talking. "What are you going to do?" she asked.

"I'm going after him," he said, charging determinedly from her room. "He's got to know that I'm still his friend."

Kernella leaped from the stool and sent it rolling over the floor as she scurried after him.

"But you can't!" she yelled, running up the passageway to the main living chamber.

Gamaliel was already climbing down the oak when she reached the entrance and popped her head outside.

"It's forbidden," she called down to him. "No one's permitted to even talk to Finnen now. Do you hear me? It's the law!"

Leaping onto the ground far below, her brother glanced up at her and shouted, "Nuts and pips to the law!"

"Gamaliel!" she cried. "Gamaliel! It's too dangerous!"

But he was not listening. Gamaliel Tumpin hurried through the woodland—heading straight for the Hagburn.

CLOSE to the oak in which the Tumpins lived, a magnificent wych elm provided dwellings for five other werling families, including the Doolans.

Sitting high in the branches, Bufus was gazing absently into space and thinking of his late brother. When Gamaliel came storming down the nearby oak, the Doolan boy heard Kernella's warning and he ground his teeth together. As well as the members of the council, he had managed to convince himself that Finnen was responsible for Mufus's death. The sight of that stupid Gammy marching off to go and speak to the despicable criminal was more than he could stand.

"No you don't, Gammy!" Bufus spat as he scrambled from his perch. "Gibble's going to know about this. He'll stop you."

# CHAPTER 14
# Betrayal

Finnen Lufkin picked his way through the dense forest, trying his best not to think about what had happened that morning. Yet still his face burned with shame. Terser Gibble had utterly humiliated him, and a stone flung by one of the Doolans' cousins had struck him painfully on the ear.

"Well, it's in the past now," he told himself. "I won't be going back there. I can't."

In the dull daylight the crowded trees did not seem quite as sinister as they had the night before, but it remained an uneasy, unsettling place. The buckled, jostling forms were even uglier now that he could see them properly. They were either bare and black or smothered in a livid lichen that was a sickly greenish color.

Above him many of the writhing, interlocked branches were still naked of bud and leaf, and their crazed limbs formed a low, cracked ceiling through which the cloud-covered sun barely penetrated. When spring eventually found its way to the forest, Finnen wondered if, after the leaves opened, a perpetual dark would descend.

*Like an endless series of caves,* he thought. *A tree-lined mine where nuggets of emerald shine in the roof on the sunniest days. Well, I've got the rest of my life to see if I'm right—if I last that long in here.*

Pensively sucking his bottom lip, he returned his full attention to the way ahead. He had been trying to find the route that the Wandering Smith had taken when he returned the werlings to their homes. Finnen was anxious to know what had happened after the Pucca had left the Silent Grove. It was a futile hope, for the Smith would most certainly have moved on, but the boy had nowhere else to go.

Pressing further into that wild realm, as the land began to rise steadily, he found that he had strayed onto the lower slopes of a hill that rose above the encompassing trees. Nettles and bracken grew over its ridges, and it was crowned by a single chestnut tree. Finnen thought it would be an excellent vantage point from which to survey the land.

Struggling through the thick weeds, he climbed to the summit and, standing on tiptoe, viewed the forest roof.

The vastness of Hagwood stretched in all directions. Glancing back westward he saw how far he had already marched. The pleasant treescape of his former home marked the edge of that ancient woodland, and beyond that was an empty wilderness that rose to the barren hills on the horizon.

It was too painful for Finnen to look on the familiar oaks of that land he had been forbidden ever to set foot on again, and so he bent his gaze south.

A sheer green wall reared up in the distance, denying any intrusion from the mobbing forest. It was the holly fence.

Finnen grimaced. There was no way he would approach that foul place again, but the Smith's camp had lain upon the far side of Frighty Aggie's gruesome abode, and so he would be forced to circle around it.

The eastern edge of Hagwood was obscured beneath a blanket of pale mist, but he thought he could discern the faint shape of some remote tower revealed in the drifting vapor.

Turning again, Finnen cast his eyes briefly to the north, where the huge green hump of the Hollow Hill dominated the skyline. Today his perception of that grassy upland was colored by the bloody histories the Smith had told him, and it appeared a menacing, brooding thing. Was the Lady Rhiannon lying dead within its halls? Surely there would be some outward sign.

A gang of crows croaked in the slate gray sky, and the boy suddenly felt alone and observed.

He had seen enough. Threading his way back down his own, humbler hill, he resumed his journey.

Keeping the holly fence as far as possible on his right, Finnen began to skirt around it. But he had not gone very far when he became aware of a great disturbance ahead.

Finnen hesitated. The forest was in uproar. There was a

din of many trampling feet crashing through the dead, stalky undergrowth, and coarse voices were braying and yelling at one another.

The werling was not close enough to understand what those brutish cries said, but he could hear the hatred behind them.

Cautiously he continued on his way, scooting from tree to tree, gradually realizing that the creators of the noise were heading his way.

All too soon Finnen caught the aggressive words, but it was still a little while before he grasped their meaning. Then, through the crooked hornbeams ahead, he saw two grotesque, briar-crested creatures lumber into sight, and knew that they could only be servants of the High Lady.

Finnen had never seen anything like the thorn ogres before, but he guessed that those monsters were responsible for Mufus's murder.

Barging their way between the trees, the ogres kept their odious faces cast to the ground. With their branching arms they parted the dead bracken and tore up turves—constantly searching and hunting.

"Seek and find it," they chanted. "Under stone—deep in hole. Seek and find it."

"Chokerstick—Krakkwhipp!" a different, shrill voice came calling from the forest behind them. "Wait by—wait by—Snaggart join—Snaggart join."

Scuttling beneath their spiky bodies, the rat-sized imp pattered forward and stamped his feet in fury.

"Snaggart not like Ungartakka!" it snapped, shaking a twiggy fist in the direction it had just scampered from.

"Ungartakka try kill Snaggart—Snaggart too fast, Snaggart jab—Ungartakka squeal!"

The small ogre laughed and waved in its claws the beautiful weapon that was the envy of the others.

Finnen saw a pale gleam in the imp's claws, but he was too far away to recognize Thimbleglaive. Snaggart had ripped the enchanted knife from the Pucca's body and claimed the blade as its very own.

"Chokerstick hate seek," one of the larger ogres growled. "Not find treasure—Chokerstick need fight, not seek."

The other rattled its branches in agreement. "Prize not here," it snarled. "Ironhead not have—not in wagon—not on him—not in bones. Krakkwhipp—he want bloodkill."

"All want bloodkill!" Snaggart snapped back. "Witchmother say go look—must be. So Snaggart do, but Snaggart not want."

A terrible realization dawned upon Finnen as he listened to the thorn ogres' horrible talk. The Wandering Smith was dead.

Sinking to the ground, Finnen covered his face. He had liked the old Pucca.

Abruptly, Snaggart jerked its pinched face to one side and flapped its ragged ears, listening. With a cry it hopped forward and dived to the soil, poking its head into a burrow. Immediately the twiglike legs began to kick while its arms engaged in a scuffle underground. A moment later it emerged, spitting fur from its mouth, and in its claws dangled the ripped shreds of a rabbit.

"Ironhead not hide treasure here," Snaggart spluttered,

burying its pinched face in the flapping skin and worrying it. "Witchmother wrong."

In the midst of his sorrow, Finnen was beset by doubt. The Smith had obviously failed in his mission. The casket containing the heart of the Lady Rhiannon was still out there somewhere, and the tyrant of the Hollow Hill would stop at nothing to retrieve it.

The werling looked up at those horrors of thorn. They had advanced a little nearer and were still grumbling about their fruitless chore. More of the monsters were foraging in the distance—he could hear the upheaval of their search-ing—and a new fear gripped him.

"She must think the box is here," he breathed. "What if She discovers that the Smith went over the Hagburn with us last night? She'll send these nightmares across. Nobody will stand a chance against them."

As silently as possible, Finnen crept from the tree and began hurrying back down his own trail. He had to return. He had to warn them.

He had run only a little distance when he rounded a patch of dead ferns and blundered blindly into a figure coming the other way.

Finnen went tumbling sideways into the undergrowth and stayed there, pale and scared, expecting a thorny claw to come reaching in for him.

The ferns rustled and were pulled roughly aside. A round face pushed its way forward and stared at him keenly.

"Hello," said Gamaliel. "You don't have to hide from me."

Finnen gaped at him, then almost laughed, but there was no time for greetings or explanations.

Hurrying from the undergrowth, he said in an urgent whisper, "Don't speak too loudly. There are enemies back there. We've got to get back and alert everyone."

"Enemies?" Gamaliel mouthed, and they both turned to run.

"Gamaliel Tumpin!" a stern voice yelled. "How dare you disobey the council's most solemn decree!"

There was Terser Gibble. As soon as Bufus Doolan had told him of Gamaliel's intent, the outraged tutor had stormed off in pursuit. Now he stood before them, glowering down his enormous nose and quivering with barely controlled wrath.

"Don't you know the depravity of this pernicious degenerate?" he bawled, pointing at Finnen. "Who are you to defy our ruling? What have you to say for yourself, you simpering toad?"

Finnen glanced back nervously. Master Gibble's shouts were resounding beneath the branches, and he was certain the thorn ogres would hear him.

"Quiet!" he hissed.

The tutor bristled and stretched himself to his full, indignant height. Angry peeps whistled from his nostrils and he yelled even louder.

"You have the audacity," he squawked, "the vulgar effrontery to order me to be silent? Your blackguardly tongue should be pulled out, you filthy, pusillanimous little barkgnawer. I am Terser Gibble, the Great Grand Wergle Master. What are you? Nothing! The dirt between my toes has more honor and worth than you."

"Whatever you say," Finnen uttered fearfully, "just so long as you shut up!"

"Please, Master Gibble!" Gamaliel implored. "You don't understand!"

The tutor would not listen.

"No, indeed!" he bellowed. "I do not understand! Never in all our history has there been such a vile, lethiferous infection as you, accursed Finnen Lufkin. The name of your family shall be wiped from our records, and the disease of your crime will be cleansed from our memories."

"Stop!" Finnen shouted anxiously.

But the harm had been done.

Just as Master Gibble drew breath, inflating himself to give vent to more scathing bile, a tremendous crashing thundered through the trees.

"Run!" Finnen cried.

Terser Gibble flicked his head left and right as they dodged around him.

"Come back here!" he commanded. "What is...?"

Then he saw them—the thorn ogres. Shrieking ferociously, they lurched into view, and the tutor of the werlings gave a strangled squeal of terror.

Whooping screeches sailed from the ogres' lips when their baleful eyes fell upon the petrified creature before them.

"Bloodkill!" Chokerstick boomed. "Bite—rend."

"Snaggart catch—Snaggart snap!" the imp crowed, trying to squeeze between them. "Snaggart want!"

Master Gibble was too stricken with horror and fear to move. The abhorrent spectacle of the marauding nightmares was beyond anything he had ever encountered, and he was rooted to the spot. Every eluding tactic and escaping maneuver froze in his brain, and his own teachings and strategies were completely forgotten.

One single, panic-free thought would wergle him into a bird and he could flee to safety in the sky; a stoat could out-run those bowed legs, a mole could delve beyond their groping reach—but no. Terser Gibble was in such a blind funk, he dithered, he clucked hopelessly, he fluttered his hands before his face, his nostrils piped a ghastly mewing—and the ogres seized him.

Krakkwhipp clapped its claws about the twitching tutor and lifted him to its widening jaws.

"Nooo!" Master Gibble screamed, thrashing his arms before the monster's repulsive face. "Help! Save me. Save me!"

Pelting up the trail, Gamaliel and Finnen heard his cries, and only then did they realize that he was not running be-hind them.

Skidding to a stop, they turned and beheld the Wergle Master's deadly plight. Up to the waiting fangs he was drawn, his shrieks gargling in his throat as the ogre's claws tightened about him.

"Finnen!" Gamaliel wailed, shielding his eyes. "I can't look!"

Courageously his friend started to run back, desperately wondering which animal shape would best serve him.

Krakkwhipp's mouth was as wide as it could stretch and Terser Gibble's long nose was already halfway inside, when suddenly Chokerstick yanked his captor's arm and the tutor was pulled into the air again.

"You not have!" Chokerstick protested. "Krakkwhipp drink much ironhead blood. Give sweetmeat to Chokerstick."

Krakkwhipp curled its dribbling lips back and wrested the branchlike arm free again.

"Krakkwhipp eat," it vowed with a threatening clack of its tongue.

Ducking beneath them and licking its own fangs when it viewed Master Gibble, Snaggart hopped and skipped before their faces.

"No bite—no eat!" the imp yapped. "Not yet—not yet! Hear it squeal—hear it squeal. Must be asked—must be asked. Owl will want—yes, it will. It say bring any with speech. Krakkwhipp must take—must take, or Witchmother will know."

"Witchmother...," the ogre moaned.

"She blast Krakkwhipp!" Chokerstick cackled. "Scorch and flame—Krakkwhipp burn!"

The ogre shuddered, and his branches clattered together in dread. Then, staring at the werling in its clutches, it grunted. "Bloodkill wait. Let owl ask—then Krakkwhipp bite."

Snaggart rubbed his own claws together. Once the messenger of the High Lady had questioned the creature, it would prize it away from Krakkwhipp with its precious little knife and see how it tasted.

With Master Gibble still whining and begging for mercy, the thorn ogres turned about and headed back through the trees.

"Spare me!" the tutor pleaded. "Spare me, please!"

Behind them, Finnen jogged to a stop and Gamaliel came puffing up to his side.

"Where are they taking him?" Kernella's brother asked. "What were those horrible things?"

Finnen shook his head. "I don't know," he murmured,

answering both questions. "But we can't just let him be carted off like that. I have to save him if I can. You go back and tell the others, I'll follow these horrors and wait for a chance."

"No, you don't, Finnen Lufkin!" Gamaliel refused. "You're going nowhere on your own. I'm coming with you."

Finnen could tell that it was pointless trying to argue, and so, as quickly as they dared, the werlings chased after the thorn ogres and pushed deeper into the forest.

Snaggart, Krakkwhipp, and Chokerstick could move swiftly on their misshapen legs. They were already out of sight but were easy enough to follow because of the shrill whistles piping from Master Gibble's nose.

Through the hornbeams, tortured elms, and malformed sycamores they stamped and stumped, while the other thorn ogres they encountered fell in behind, laughing at the terrified notes sounding from the puny creature they had caught.

In the wake of this mustering host, Gamaliel and Finnen began to despair. There were so many of those disgusting monsters that they could never hope to liberate Master Gibble. The thought of abandoning him, however, never once entered their thoughts, and they continued pursuing the servants of Rhiannon until finally they came to where the Smith had made his encampment.

A terrible violence had been visited upon that small space. The devastation was absolute: Trees were thrown down, their roots unearthed and exposed, and the trunks were hacked and torn apart. Deep pits and trenches had been gouged in the soil, and more were being dug. It was as if an infernal tempest had fallen upon that one part of

Hagwood and spent its full, squalling might within those limited confines. Not a blade of grass was left standing or unbroken, and even the stones were cracked like eggs.

To this desolation the thorn ogres came barging, pouring over the splintered trees to gather around the brinks of the newly grubbed pits. Jostling and shoving one another, they bayed and barked, eager to see what the messenger of the High Lady would make of the unusual creature in Krakkwhipp's claws.

Cautiously, Gamaliel and Finnen approached. They could not believe what their senses were showing them. Destruction on such a scale was outside the experience or knowledge of any werling. Finnen's throat went dry when he thought about a calamity of equal force striking in the heart of their home beyond the Hagburn.

"What's happened here?" Gamaliel whispered, keeping well out of sight. "Is this really where the Pucca brought us?"

Finnen made no answer. It was vital that they saw what was happening in the middle of that clamoring crowd, but it was impossible to see past the stout, buckled legs and trailing, spiky tails. For a moment he toyed with the idea of wergling into a bird and spying on them from above, but even as he raised his eyes, he saw that one of the uprooted trees was leaning directly over that hideous multitude.

Murmuring his plan to Gamaliel, they sneaked across the shattered ground and climbed nimbly up the ravaged trunk as far as they could without being spotted, then peered down.

In the center of that malevolent crew, a large barn owl was perched on a pile of twisted metal: the mangled remains of the Wandering Smith's wares. And even as the werlings gazed upon that frightful scene, Krakkwhipp offered up Master Gibble for the bird's inspection.

The owl blinked its golden eyes and stared at the quivering tutor contemptuously.

"Have pity!" Master Gibble squealed, believing the ogres were about to feed him to the bird. "Don't kill me! Don't give me to that mouse-eater, I beseech you! Let me go free! Please!"

The snowy feathers ruffled and the owl clicked its beak.

Master Gibble threw his hands before his face. "No! No!" he yowled with every nostril blaring.

"Why do ye bring this paltry runt before me?" the owl demanded.

"It spoke!" the werling cried in wild consternation. "An owl that speaks! Beeches take me, I have gone quite mad."

The bird flexed its talons and hunched its wings. "'Tis naught but a wer-rat," it remarked. "A lowly, base creation of no import."

Krakkwhipp mumbled and shifted morosely.

"Snaggart have!" the imp at its side demanded, jumping up and down impatiently.

Krakkwhipp shoved Snaggart away and slobbered hungrily.

"Hold!" the owl shouted suddenly. "Show me the wer-rat once more."

Master Gibble was waved in front of the bird's face again, and the tutor gibbered pathetically.

"Yea," the owl said softly. "Gofannon, the arch traitor did speak with four of these puny creatures, this ender night ere he perished. Could it be that my Lady's servants hath hunted in the wrong places for that thing he stole?"

The golden eyes closed, and the bird sang quietly under its breath.

"Mistress of the twilight," it intoned. "Hear the supplication of thy humble Provost."

Far away, in the deep caverns beneath the Hollow Hill, the Lady Rhiannon took up a silver mask fashioned and graven into the shape of an owl's face, and placed it before her own ravishing countenance.

Upon the wreckage of the Smith's wares, a purling sigh floated from the owl's beak, and the icy draught was like the very breath of winter.

"Where is this one you would have Us behold?" the bird said, but the voice that spoke was not its own, and when the eyes opened, bright silver shone where previously only gold had burned.

"Witchmother!" the ogres groaned, cowering and fawning on the ground.

An argent gleam flickered over their thorny features, and they cringed and hid their horrendous faces. Finally the cold light fell upon Terser Gibble, and the spindly werling stammered and wept.

"Lowbred beast," came the bitter voice of the Lady Rhiannon. "Hear the dictate of your Queen and obey Us without question."

Master Gibble wagged his head, trilling incessantly through his nose. "Anything!" he swore.

The pale light flared. "Where is the casket that was stolen? To what secret place did Gofannon bear it? Where is it bestowed? You will tell Us. You must answer!"

"C-casket?" the tutor stuttered. "Wh-what?"

A despising glitter sparkled in the silver depths. "That

most valuable treasure which the treacherous Smith did steal!" the harsh voice snapped. "Where is it?"

Master Gibble quaked and shook, and his frantic whistles became ever shriller. "I-I don't...I don't know any...of any...I just..."

"The wer-rat knows nothing!" the voice scorned. "You waste our time, Provost. Destroy this puling creature, feed him to our pets."

"Noooo!" Master Gibble shrieked as the silver light began to fade and he strove to save himself. What was the Wandering Smith to him? Nothing, a dirty, beggarly creature of the big folk. Why should he, the Great Grand Wergle Master, die because of one such as he?

"I think—yes, I do know something!" he cried.

"You lie!" came the fierce response. "We read you right, tiny wheedler. All your thoughts are for your quailing skin; you would say aught to spare it."

The tutor nodded feverishly. "Yes!" he cried. "Indeed, I would, but I do know of what you speak. That one you named the Smith—he was seen in my land—I saw him myself."

Brilliantly now the eyes blazed, and Master Gibble nearly swooned from the glare of them. "Is that where the casket lies?" the voice rang out.

"I know not!" the werling replied, anxious to appease. "But I am certain of the one who would know. He was in the Smith's company longer than any, and many words they exchanged. On my life I swear it. If any might know where this thing you so justly want returned may be, it's him—Finnen Lufkin!"

Watching in the tree above, Finnen stared down at the

wretched Terser Gibble, bewildered and afraid. He could not believe how drastically the tutor had changed. Robbed of his authority and under the threat of death, the once-pompous Wergle Master had degenerated into a pathetic, whining creature. He had divulged the boy's name to the enemy almost eagerly. What would the cowardly tutor say next? Just how far would he go in order to deliver himself from the power of Rhiannon?

"He's the one!" Master Gibble gabbled on. "A most untrustworthy, ungrateful child is Finnen Lufkin. He'll know, I'm sure of it!"

The owl regarded him doubtfully, and the werling's whistling notes dwindled to forsaken, jarring chirps.

"It's the truth, I promise!" he cried. "How can I prove it to you? How?"

A dark glimmer of his own entered the tormented tutor's beady eyes, and a fey laugh giggled from his mouth.

"I know!" he crowed as his last fragment of courage finally disintegrated. "The Great Grand Wergle Master knows!"

Flinging his arms wide, he tossed back his head and yelled, "Send your fiendish pets over the Hagburn, my most honored Lady! They will be met by the doughty forces of my people, who will resist with every trick they know, everything I have taught them."

"They will be slain," the voice declared without emotion.

"Not without a fight!" he hooted. "But spare my life and there will be no contest, none whatsoever. I guarantee! Heed me now and my folk can be defeated and captured; the treasure you seek will be won more swiftly."

The wintry light glimmered over the werling's face.

"Dearly do you buy your spineless life, yet if this is true then you have earned your freedom of Us."

Master Gibble clasped his hands and sniveled his gratitude, while his nostrils twittered unharmoniously. Then the most respected and revered member of the werling race committed the most despicable and loathsome sin in the long history of their kind.

It was the vilest, absolute and unrepentant betrayal, yet Terser Gibble laughed when he uttered it. Every one of his high, haughty ideals had vanished, and only the all-consuming need to survive and keep his own detestable skin remained.

"This is how you conquer them!" he proclaimed.

*"Amwin par cavirrien sul, olgun forweth, i rakundor.*
*Skarta nen skila cheen,*
*Emar werta i fimmun-lo.*
*Perrun lanssa dirifeen, tatha titha Dunwrach."*

Listening to his words from their position in the tree, Gamaliel and Finnen stared at each other in horror. It was far, far worse than Finnen's own crime. Compared with this ultimate treachery, the stealing of wood from the Silent Grove paled into oblivion.

"The passwords! How could he?" Gamaliel breathed. "He's told them the secret unlocking passwords!"

Aghast, Finnen shuddered. "We have to get back," he whispered. "Gibble's saved his own neck; now it's up to us to save the others. We haven't a moment to lose."

Pleased with his craven cunning, Master Gibble instructed

the servants of the High Lady until the ancient words were learned.

"None shall withstand them," he said proudly. "You said I could go free."

The silver eyes gleamed at him. "And so you may," the voice promised. The owl turned its head to Krakkwhipp, ordering the monster to let the wer-rat loose.

The thorn ogre lowered its claw, but the bird's beak opened once more, and before their mistress removed the silver mask from her face in the Hollow Hill, she added maliciously, "Verily you must turn him loose, but not until you have separated the base creature from his irritating nose. Cut it off!"

With the agonized screams of Master Gibble ringing in their ears, Gamaliel and Finnen scurried down the trunk and ran for their lives.

But as they sped from that devastation, one of the thorn ogres chanced to turn and it saw them flee.

"Spies!" it croaked. "See—spies!"

Every foul head ranged around to stare, and the bleak voice of the Lady Rhiannon called, "After them! To battle, my pets! To battle!"

Shrieking and screeching, the evil host charged forth.

# CHAPTER 15
# Jumbled

Hideous shouts blared beneath the trees, and the forest streaked past Gamaliel and Finnen as a tangled blur.

Away from the mutilation of the Smith's encampment they pelted, running as fast as they could, but Gamaliel could not keep up with Finnen.

"Quickly!" Finnen cried, spurring his plump friend on.

"I can't!" Gamaliel huffed.

The whooping din of the pursuing thorn ogres was growing steadily louder, but even that could not make Gamaliel's legs move any faster.

"They're gaining on us!" Finnen exclaimed. "Hurry, Gamaliel—you must!"

Through the strangling trees they lunged, but all the while the ferocious, trumpeting shrieks of the High Lady's servants mounted, and their pounding feet caused the ground to shake.

"It's no use!" Finnen yelled above the racketing riot. "We'll have to wergle into something faster."

Gamaliel's legs were aching and his chest was tight and painful. "No!" he cried. "I can't. You know I can't! I've never even changed into a mouse. You go on, Finnen. I should never have come. Leave me here. Go tell the others."

"No one's going to be left anywhere!" Finnen replied. "All I have to do is wergle into a bird strong enough to carry you, and we'll both be safe."

The ogres were almost upon them; they could hear the clatter of their thorny branches. Finnen leaped into the air, spreading his arms and flapping them.

With a lurch he fell. There were no feathers, no wings—the wergling had not taken place.

Shocked and fearful, he bolted upright and tried again. Jumping high, he concentrated hard and ground his teeth together, squeezing his eyes tight shut and believing himself to be a bird.

Nothing happened, and he landed with a judder.

Finnen's face blanched, and he tried a third time. Finally he turned to Gamaliel and in a scared voice declared, "I can't do it. Without the wood from the Silent Grove I can't wergle into anything!"

"What are we to do?" Gamaliel wept.

The thorn ogres were crashing through the trees behind

them. The werlings could see their pale eyes shining fiercely, and in the sky above, the barn owl was squawking its orders.

Finnen looked around wildly. The hill topped by a single chestnut tree was not far away, and he gripped Gamaliel by the shoulders.

"Listen to me!" he demanded. "It's up to you now. You've got to do this on your own."

"But I'm not as fast as you!" came the wretched reply.

"Neither of us is fast enough the way we are!" Finnen shouted. "I can't wergle, so you must!"

"Me?" Gamaliel wailed. "It's impossible."

"No, it's not!" Finnen yelled, shaking him. "You can do this, I know you can. You have to; you're our only hope!"

"But what about you?"

Finnen pointed to the hill. "If I can reach that," he said doubtfully, "I might be able to hide. But it doesn't matter, only you do. Go warn the others, tell them what Gibble's done. Don't stop to worry about me; there isn't time."

Tears pricked Gamaliel's eyes. He stared at the stampeding nightmares that were now only a short distance away and were reaching with their claws.

"Forget them!" Finnen commanded. "Do it, Gamaliel! For all our sakes!"

Trembling, and with the clamor of the enemy roaring behind him, Gamaliel Tumpin opened his wergle pouch.

Uncertainly, he reached into the velvety bag. It was still stuffed with odds and ends, and he drew out a matted clump of fur, bristles, and feathers.

"It's all mixed up!" he howled. "I don't even know which is the mouse's."

"Just do it!" Finnen told him.

Gamaliel closed his eyes, thrust the untidy mess under his nose, and took one great, despairing sniff.

Stars exploded in the werling's mind. His skin crackled and fizzed, and his body was wracked by vicious spasms as mighty forces gripped him. He was wergling.

But not all the venom of Frighty Aggie's sting had been drawn from his shoulder. Traces still lingered, and they conferred strange powers upon young Gamaliel Tumpin.

The bones of his legs creaked and stretched, buckling into those of a young hare. A sleek coat of ginger fur sprouted all over his face, and his hands became squirrel paws. From the top of his snookulhood burst a crown of feathers, and his jerkin ripped and tore when hedgehog spines came thrusting from his back. With a final jolt, a mouse's tail snaked out behind, and Gamaliel blinked in surprise.

Finnen gawped at him.

Gamaliel was a bizarre mishmash of creatures. It went against every known wergling law.

"What's happened?" Finnen asked. "You're a bit of everything. It's incredible! Nobody can do that! Are you all right?"

Gamaliel nodded hastily and hopped upon his new legs. "I think I can make it!" he cried. "I feel strong and swift."

"Then run!" Finnen called, for at that moment the ogres came rushing to snatch them.

Off Gamaliel shot, bounding and leaping over the dead bracken, traveling faster than he ever had dreamed. Into his ears the wind went coursing, and the feathers on the top of his head waved madly as he raced along.

Finnen could not begin to match the speed of his friend's new mongrel shape, and he fell rapidly behind. But the ogres were still clutching at his heels, and when he reached the lower slopes of the nettle-covered hill, he darted aside and shot up into the weeds.

Like an avalanche of briar and bramble, the monsters rumbled by, yammering at the top of their rasping voices, calling for death and murder.

Not daring to pause, Finnen scaled the hill, and when he reached the summit, he clambered quickly up into the chestnut tree.

Breathless and spent, he perched upon one of the lower branches and stared down at the forest roof. Through the twining boughs he saw the surging horde flood through Hagwood, heading unerringly for the land of the werlings. Above them the barn owl circled, and Finnen hoped that Gamaliel's new shape would not fail him.

"Good luck," he murmured.

At the base of the tree a small figure came crashing through the nettles and cackled to itself when it saw Finnen hiding in the branches.

"Snaggart want," it crooned, and licking its fangs, the imp began to climb.


THE weird, jumbled creature that was Gamaliel raced through the forest like the wind.

He had already put a great distance between himself and the army of the High Lady, but the thorn ogres were no longer his most immediate problem.

Swooping from the sky, the owl dived at Gamaliel's head with its talons outstretched to hook into his skull. Gamaliel could feel the furious downdraft of the great wings, and the bird's shadow deepened about him. At the last moment, the werling hunched over, and the owl's feet went grasping at his sharp hedgehog spines.

The owl screeched with punctured rage and soared up once more, only to wheel about and plummet for a second attack. Again Gamaliel curled up, but this time the bird was calling out, and he shuddered with fright when he heard.

"*Amwin par cavirrien sul,*" the owl declaimed, "*olgun forweth, i rakundor.*"

Down it dived, and the secret passwords were bawled from its beak.

"*Skarta nen skila cheen, emar werta i fimmun-lo.*"

Gamaliel held his breath and bit his lip, expecting his shape to melt away.

"*Perrun lanssa dirifeen, tatha titha Dunwrach.*"

That was it. Gamaliel heard the rush of wings and waited for the protecting hedgehog spines to vanish. But, to his delight and amazement, he remained exactly the same and unchanged. The ancient unlocking charm had been devised only for known forms, and over the hybrid creature he had wergled into they had no power.

Above him the owl squawked in impotent fury, and Gamaliel sprang away, his rabbit's feet barely touching the ground.

The owl continued to harry him, but Gamaliel was confident now, and he hurtled along in an insane zigzag that baffled the bird's plunging talons. Then to his joy he saw the banks of the Hagburn appear before him, and without a second's delay the long legs launched him from the edge.

Across the stream he vaulted, springing up as soon as he landed upon the other side.

"'Ware! 'Ware!" he hollered. "Wolves! Owls! Witches! 'Ware! 'Ware!"

Into the land of the werlings he raced, and the old alarm cry brought dozens of faces crowding to the entrances of their homes in the trees.

"What is it?" they called, gazing at the peculiar creature hurrying below and observing with dread the barn owl that was still dive-bombing and hounding it. "Who's down there?"

"It's me!" the uncanny beast yelled. "Gamaliel! Gamaliel Tumpin!"

He sped to the oak where his family lived, and his father was already scuttling down to meet him.

A stout stick was in Figgle Tumpin's fist, and when the owl lunged for his son he leaped up and smote it across the leg.

"Get gone, you foul flappy thing!" he shouted. "Or I'll have your feathers in a pillow and you in a roast!"

The bird shrieked at him and thrashed its wings to hover in the air as it slashed and raked with its claws.

A fierce scratch cut across Figgle's cheek, and he battered his stick in the owl's face.

The messenger of Rhiannon screeched, but now many other werlings were running to the Tumpins' aid, and both Tidubelle and Kernella were hurling stones from Gamaliel's collection as they scampered along the branches above.

With a mighty thrust of its wings, the owl shot into the sky, accompanied by sticks, pebbles, and rude shouts, then moved off over the trees toward the forest.

"That's got rid of it!" the small folk cheered. "What's it doing out in the daytime anyway? Daft loony."

A large number of werlings had gathered about the roots of the Tumpins' oak. Liffidia was there, as well as Tollychook. Everyone was agog to know what was going on and just what had happened to Gamaliel.

"Look at him!" they gasped. "Whatever is it? It's not natural—downright fright'nin'."

Gulping for breath, Gamaliel was trying to explain to his father when Yoori Mattock came pushing through the throng.

"What in Hagwood are you supposed to be?" he demanded sternly. "You're a disgrace, lad. An abominable-nation."

"Don't you speak to our Gamaliel like that!" Figgle cried, shoving Mr. Mattock in the chest.

"And don't you push me!" Yoori told him. "You should be ashamed of your—"

"Stop it!" Gamaliel yelled. "There are enemies coming. Huge monsters. You have to arm yourselves, find whatever weapons you can. They'll kill you, kill you all!"

A ghastly hush followed his feverish words, and the werlings looked at one another fearfully.

"Monsters?" Yoori Mattock said, not believing a word.

"Yes!" Gamaliel answered defiantly. "They caught Master Gibble and he betrayed us. He told them the passwords. Poor Finnen's stuck, back in the forest. He could be dead by now for all I know or you care...Listen!"

The rumor of a tremendous uproar was rising from beyond the Hagburn. Flocks of birds, frightened from their nests, took to the air, swirling through the sky like dense clouds. The werlings murmured in dismay.

"Monsters...," they whispered.

Yoori Mattock stared at Gamaliel and realized the boy was speaking the truth. Apologies would have to wait. There was very little time to organize themselves, but as the leader of the presiding council, Mr. Mattock instantly took command.

"Make certain everyone has heard the alarm!" he announced, turning to the frightened werlings. "Do as the lad says. Arm yourselves. We will meet this foe at our borders."

In every corner of the normally tranquil woodland, the alarm was called. Within minutes a great number of the shape-changers were striding toward the stream, bearing sticks and knives. Most of them had wergled into fierce animal forms: rats, weasels, ferrets, and stoats, but none of them suspected what manner of horror they were about to encounter.

The horrendous bellowing of the enemy was closer now, and as they converged upon the brink of the Hagburn, the werlings steeled themselves for the coming battle.

Still wearing his mongrel shape, Gamaliel watched the hasty preparations with Kernella. Figgle and Tidubelle had joined the ranks of the defenders, and the children felt woefully small and helpless as the tension swelled and the unholy tumult set the oaks to shivering.

The enemy was almost upon them. Their violent, bloodthirsty yells were awful to hear. Several werlings found the encroaching terror unbearable and fled from the bank, squealing. But the rest remained steadfast and resolute.

Then the storm broke.

From the forest the thorn ogres came savaging. Over the Hagburn they leaped, and the battle began.

Daunted by the gruesome appearance of the immense

creatures, the werlings cried out, but they stood their ground, and when the ogres attacked, they threw themselves upon them.

Chaos erupted. Wergled claws drove into woody flesh and sharp teeth sank deep into the invaders' horrendous faces. Yet against the army of Rhiannon, such assaults were vain and futile. Stoats and ferrets were dragged from the nightmares' heads by the ogres' more vicious claws. They were flung to the ground, where clubbed feet smashed and crushed them.

Eight werlings were killed in the first skirmish, but still the others fought, meeting the enemy with monumental courage. More of them perished, and then the ogres began to chant, droning in their malevolent, hollow voices the secret passwords. When the last phrase was uttered, the brief conflict was ended.

Weasels, rats, and ferrets immediately disappeared. Robbed of their fierce guises, the werlings howled in distress. From the branching bodies of the thorn ogres they slid, falling in terror before the cackling fiends, who snatched and seized them—throttling and rending with wanton malice.

"Flee!" Yoori Mattock cried. "To the trees! To the trees!"

Away from the Hagburn the shape-changers ran. Some of them still attempted to wergle into agile forms, only to be thwarted by the reciting of the unlocking words. Those who failed to make it to the lofty shelters were cruelly dealt with. Murdered victims were impaled on spiky branches, and the macabre trophies drew grief-stricken screams from their fleeing families.

Into the nearest trees the werlings scrambled, crowding along the branches and praying that the monsters could not climb. Pursued by Chokerstick, Figgle and Tidubelle barely managed to gain their oak in time. Even as they darted up the trunk, a barbed claw lashed out and missed them by a whisker.

Incensed, Chokerstick bellowed, and lowering its repugnant head, butted the bole of the Tumpin oak. A ruinous shudder traveled up the towering tree, and Figgle yowled as his toes lost their grip on the bark.

"Don't you dare, my love!" Tidubelle scolded, reaching across to save and support him.

But not all were so fortunate.

Other werlings were thrown off balance and fell, shrieking, to their deaths, while those who had not reached the safety of the trees were slaughtered on the ground.

Petrified and sobbing, Tollychook was too far from any hope of reaching sanctuary. Tripping over his large feet and blinded by tears, he was stumbling through the fallen leaves when a huge shadow swamped him.

Down came an immense, slavering head, and the narrow eyes lit upon Tollychook's round figure greedily.

"No!" the werling boy blubbered. "Go away. Please, no!"

Two branching arms swung around to trap him, and Tollychook bleated piteously.

"Bloodkill," the unclean voice gloated.

Whimpering, Tollychook felt the stinking breath beat upon his face.

A ferocious barking suddenly sounded, and from nowhere Liffidia's fox cub came rushing up to clamp its jaws about the thorn ogre's arm.

The monster snarled and lumbered backward, rearing on its stunted legs to shake the animal off.

A night's peaceful rest to forget the horrors of Frighty Aggie, coupled with loving attention from Liffidia, had worked a miracle on the fox. It was stronger now, but still no opponent for one of Rhiannon's infernal pets.

With a yelp the cub was tossed aside. It ran off through the woodland with its tail between its legs.

But the distraction had been enough.

Liffidia had darted in to rescue Tollychook from the monster's clutches, and they were already scaling the nearest tree.

"Thank you!" Tollychook burbled. "I was nearly eated!"

In the Tumpin oak, Gamaliel and his family watched them climb into the wych elm where the Doolans lived, and heaved glad, grateful sighs. But the threat was far from over.

Far below, Chokerstick wearied of ramming its head against the trunk and hooked its claws into the bark. The thorny branches rattled, and it heaved itself off the ground. All through the woodland the ogres were clambering up, and there was nowhere for the werlings to run to.

"We're done for!" Figgle breathed.

# CHAPTER 16
# The Battle of the Trees

**B**eyond the Hagburn, Finnen Lufkin was facing a peril of his own.

In the branches of the chestnut tree, Snaggart was hunting him. Gurgling with wicked relish, the imp crawled up the trunk.

"Sweet—fangsome dainty," it muttered. "Snaggart want—Snaggart bite."

Finnen had nothing with which to defend himself. Desperately he tried to wergle, but his marvelous gift had derived solely from the wood of the Silent Grove, and without it he was powerless. The only thing he could do was climb and try to evade Snaggart's claws for as long as possible. Running to the hill had been a stupid and reckless idea. The chestnut tree stood tall and alone above the forest. There were no other trees to leap across to—and no escape.

"Stay away from me!" he yelled.

Higher the ratlike thorn ogre crept. Its malevolent eyes swiveled in its sharp face, intently following Finnen's frantic movements as he scurried out of reach.

"Crunch bone—drink blood," it taunted. "Snaggart catch."

The disgraced werling climbed faster until he came to a junction in the trunk, where three mighty boughs reached out almost horizontally, their radiating branches meeting to form a precarious platform that encircled the tree's girth. Onto the greatest branch Finnen ran, and Snaggart jumped on behind him.

"Chase and kill!" the imp snickered.

Along the spreading limb Finnen hurried, nimbly dashing over that dividing route and hopping across the empty gulfs between the branches.

But Snaggart was just as agile, and the ogre reveled in the deadly game. Round and round the trunk it pursued the frightened werling boy. Then it switched direction without warning to go scampering about the other way, so that Finnen would suddenly encounter it bounding before him.

"Begone!" Finnen cried. "Leave me!"

The imp mocked his fearful calls and, with malicious glee, decided to make its play more amusing. Wielding the Smith's enchanted knife, Snaggart began to chop away the connecting branches after scurrying across them. Finnen found the winding way becoming increasingly impassable.

Finally he was stranded on one of the three main boughs with nowhere to run except back toward the trunk. But before he could reach it, Snaggart came leaping over, and the imp stood blocking his retreat.

In its claws the ogre flicked the knife to and fro. "Snaggart stop chasey," it growled. "Snaggart want—Snaggart jab—Snaggart bite."

Along the branch the ogre came stalking, a horrid, hungry light in its eyes. Finnen edged away as far as he dared.

"Don't you come any closer!" he warned, and the ridiculous, empty threat made Snaggart cackle all the louder.

The narrowing limb began to bounce and sag beneath them, and a daring, foolhardy idea flooded into Finnen's mind.

Lifting his gaze, he made the decision and jumped up, coming down again with all his weight on the springing branch. The timbers creaked and the slender way dipped horrendously. Snaggart yelped and held on grimly, then up the branch sprang, and Finnen shot high into the twigs above.

"Slippy cheater!" Snaggart yapped, shaking its fists. "Snaggart snatch—Snaggart rip!"

Clinging to the twigs, Finnen stared down at the furious imp then hurried toward the trunk.

Below him, Snaggart copied his movements. It had had its fun and now the hunt was in earnest.

Up it climbed, the knife clenched between its fangs. Finnen would not evade it any longer.

To the top of the chestnut tree the werling hastened, until at last there was nowhere left to run to. He was trapped in the uppermost branches, where only a pair of wings could save him.

Snaggart drew the blade from its jaws and prowled nearer. The imp was horribly close, and Finnen knew that he was about to die.

"Snappy snappy," the thorn ogre hissed. "Snaggart chew—Snaggart crunch."

It inched its way toward the despairing boy, savoring the terror written across its victim's face. A brown tongue flicked over Snaggart's cracked lips, and it shivered with delicious anticipation.

Finnen had backed away as far as he could without falling from that hideous height. But it would be better to end his life that way. A quick plunge to death was more preferable than being devoured by that loathsome devil.

The world of Hagwood spread far below like a boundless map, and Finnen prepared to jump.

"No!" Snaggart snapped, guessing the thoughts of its prey. "Bloodkill."

With that, the ogre pounced, and Finnen shrieked.

But Snaggart squealed even louder, for as it leaped at the werling, a gigantic claw reached up from beneath, and the imp was yanked backward.

Kicking and screaming, and with the Smith's knife flying from its grasp, Snaggart was dragged down through the branches—to a pair of waiting, clicking jaws.

There was Frighty Aggie. Her monstrous, jointed legs were wrapped about the trunk, and her many eyes were fixed upon Finnen.

Stupefied, the werling stared at her while, emitting one last squeal, Snaggart was bitten in half and eaten.

The horror that dwelt behind the holly fence twisted its enormous head, and the thin laugh that Finnen remembered all too clearly blistered across the forest.

Returning her baleful attention to the boy, the ghastly voice fell silent, and a pale gleam flickered in the depths of her countless eyes.

Finnen understood.

In those fragmented clusters he saw a thousand distorted reflections of himself and realized just how close he had come to a doom like hers. To chew the wood of the Silent Grove was a perilous gamble. He could easily have suffered the same fate as she.

Twice now she had spared his life, for in the unlit regions of her insect mind she recognized that there was a bond between them. She knew it, that night outside her lair, when she sensed the strong link they shared.

"You heard me cry out," Finnen said, and he no longer feared her. "Just now, you heard my voice and knew I was in danger. You came to help me because we're...we were the same. I'm like you, like what you were before. I made the same terrible mistake."

The abhorrent nightmare regarded him almost tenderly, as a mother might a son, but the only sound was the click of her awful jaws.

"Thank you," the boy murmured.

A faint rattling noise echoed in her throat, then down the tree her eight legs carried her.

Watching her descend then creep back toward the holly fence, Finnen knew that he had been immensely lucky. So far he had escaped the obscene torment that had consumed Agnilla Hellekin. Up there in the topmost branches of the chestnut tree he made a solemn promise to himself. Never again would he set foot in the werling burial ground.

Finnen turned his gaze to the land of his home. What evil destruction were the thorn ogres wreaking there?

Swallowing nervously, he commenced the long climb down.

IN STEADY, lurching movements, the hulking shape of Chokerstick scaled the Tumpin oak. Throughout that woodland the murderous forces of Rhiannon were hoisting themselves up into the trees while the owl swooped down, demanding the surrender of the one called Finnen Lufkin.

But no answer did the bird receive, for the battle of the trees had begun.

Kernella and Tidubelle had ransacked the Tumpin home in search of weapons, but the only useful item was an old spear that Figgle took with him on his mole hunts. Gamaliel brought out the last of his pebble collection and piled the stones about the entrance in readiness. Yet they all knew that it would take more than these humble objects to defend themselves.

The Dritch family, who lived below, was slightly better equipped. They had two bows and three dozen arrows, but their neighbor, old Mistress Woonak, possessed no weapons at all and feebly brandished her knitting needles.

Up came Chokerstick, and the Dritches fired a volley of arrows at its hideous face. The tips of four arrows bit into the ogre's woody hide, but the rest simply bounced off. A repulsive, bragging laugh rumbled in the monster's gullet, and quickening its pace, the malignant brute drew level with the entrance to the Dritches' home.

Seeing it approach, the werlings had fled inside, but Chokerstick reached in with its long barbed arm, and harrowing screams issued from within.

When the arm withdrew, it was dripping with blood. Chokerstick lapped it like a cat at cream, then the barbarous creature started to climb once more, smearing a crimson trail in its wake.

Hearing the deaths of the family below, the werlings who were gathered outside the Tumpin dwelling felt sick. Still wearing his bizarre shape, Gamaliel watched the fiend approach.

"It's nearly here!" he called.

Gripping the spear grimly, Figgle readied himself, and each of the others took a pebble from the entrance.

Up over the branches the clattering, thorny crown of the ogre reared, swiftly followed by its craggy brows and then the pale, almost white eyes that roved rapaciously over the cowering werlings.

"Come," it croaked. "Give to Chokerstick—blood sweet."

At once a hail of stones was pelted at the repugnant face, but the monster felt nothing. The puny missiles ricocheted harmlessly off its tough, woody skin, and the ghastly eyes watched in foul amusement when the small, frightened creatures had no more stones to throw and began to squeal all the louder.

The ogre's great, drooling lips opened wide to hiss with laughter.

Suddenly, yelling at the top of his voice, Figgle Tumpin lunged forward and hurled the spear into the gaping mouth.

"Get off my doorstep!" he hollered.

Down the cavernous throat the spear went flying, and the ogre convulsed in pain. Roaring, it slid down the trunk, but its claws gouged deep into the bark and held it fast. Wheezing and rasping, the monster hauled itself up once more, and the malformed face was twisted with wrath.

Hate and malice burned in those narrow eyes more fiercely than ever, and Chokerstick came storming over the branch to tear Figgle apart.

Mr. Tumpin stumbled to get away, but the shadow fell across him and the grotesque head descended.

Suddenly a prickly shape jumped between them, and leaping backward, Gamaliel thrust his hedgehog spikes into the ravening face.

Chokerstick screamed. The sharp bristles had pierced one of the squinting eyes, and the ogre fell from the branch, toppling out of the tree.

Flailing its mighty arms and bellowing in fear, the thorn ogre tumbled through the air. Upside down it plummeted. Then, with a juddering crunch, the ogre smashed onto the ground.

The thicket that grew from the horror's humped back rammed deeply into the soil, and Chokerstick kicked its deformed legs at the sky to right itself. But the branching thorns anchored it to the earth, and it was stuck fast.

High above, the werlings cheered, watching it struggle and writhe in fury. But they had not realized that a second ogre had scaled their oak. Even as they cast their gazes upon

Chokerstick's frenzied efforts, Ungartakka was lifting its mountainous head behind them.

In the surrounding trees many more deadly confrontations were taking place. The unhallowed legion of the High Lady's army had proved victorious. Nothing could withstand the ogres' malevolent attacks, and the woodland trembled to the clamor of their hideous shouts.

Nowhere was safe from their prowling slaughter. Beneath those canopies of bright new leaves the werlings were cornered, and their death screams rang from tree to tree.

Only the stoutest hearts endeavored to battle the thorn-crested devils. In the wych elm of the Doolans, Yoori Mattock was wielding an old ceremonial sword and had supplied the bravest of the others with long knives. Liffidia, Tollychook, Bufus, and four other children were sent to the highest branches as three large ogres came clambering up the trunk. On the lower boughs, Mr. Mattock and his valiant group formed a line of defense. But their knees were quaking, and the hands that held the weapons shook from the monumental fear that gripped them.

"Stand firm!" Yoori called. "We can't let one of them by us. Fight or die! Fight or die!"

Higher the ogres climbed, and when the first malformed finger came reaching over the branch where he stood, Mr. Mattock pounced upon it, hacking with the sword and yelling at the top of his voice.

The finger splintered and was sliced in two, but it only made the monster below snarl more viciously. When it pulled its hulking body level with the werlings, the ogre's fangs were eagerly snapping and champing.

Onto the bough it hauled itself. At once Yoori sprang forward, slashing and slicing so wildly that for a moment the monster was confounded.

Up into the grotesque snout the sword blade jabbed, and the tip of an unclean, misshapen nose was sent spinning to the ground. The ogre roared and slammed its fist against the trunk, causing the whole tree to shiver. But Mr. Mattock had not finished, and several of his companions had rallied to his side.

With their knives they stabbed up at the vile creature's throat, and it backed away over the branch, gurgling horribly. The ravaging claws went swiping for those nasty little insects with their bitterly sharp points, but they hopped and dodged, and always their blades came cutting and carving.

Further along the narrowing branch, the werlings drove it, until there was a rending crack, and the wood split beneath the horror's awful weight.

From the wych elm the ogre fell, but even as it toppled, its grasping claws lashed out and caught Yoori across his head. Unable to save himself, Mr. Mattock went tumbling after the plunging nightmare, and the sword slipped from his grasp.

From the top of the tree, Liffidia and the other children watched them fall and felt the tremendous crash when the ogre hit the ground. Tollychook winced and hid his face.

"Poor Mr. Mattock!" he wailed.

Liffidia shook him by the arm. "No!" she cried. "It's all right; he's not hurt."

Peering down, they saw that Yoori had broken his fall

by grabbing on to the twigs of the lowest branches and had swung himself safely to the woodland floor.

Tollychook brightened for an instant, then realized that the ogre was also unharmed. The thorns had been snapped from its back, but already it was staggering onto its clubbed feet once more.

Yoori had no time to climb back into the tree. Maddened beyond fury, the monster went screaming toward him, and the werling could only turn and run.

"Faster, Mr. Mattock!" Tollychook cried. "It's a-gainin' on you!"

Behind the Tumpin oak the leader of the council fled, with the thorn ogre charging straight after him.

"Did he make it?" Tollychook asked fretfully.

Liffidia did not answer, for she had glanced directly below them to where Krakkwhipp and another grotesque creature were dealing with the rest of the defenders.

This time the werlings could not hope to win. The ogres ignored the cuts from their knives. Their brutal onslaught was aided by the revulsion that overcame their small opponents as they faced the terrible ogres—a revulsion that weakened their stabbing thrusts.

Not one of them could bear to look at Krakkwhipp, for upon the fiend's spikes were impaled many of those who had perished in the first skirmish. The gruesome spectacle was too harrowing to witness, and Krakkwhipp gurgled with hellish mirth to see them so affected by its delicious dangling ornaments. Taunting them, the depraved monster shook its head from side to side, and the limp little corpses that it wore swung and swayed to its ghastly rhythm.

Aghast and repulsed, the werlings threw their knives at it. Then they ran, only to be captured by the second ogre. Into its massive claws most of them were swept and swiftly shoveled inside the immense, fang-filled mouth.

Only a few of the defenders managed to escape. They scrambled up to where the children were perched, and the enemies came creeping after.

From every tree a crimson rain began to fall, and swooping between them, the owl became filled with doubt and dismay.

This was not the strategy of the Lady Rhiannon. A swift attack to subdue all resistance was what She had instructed. When that was accomplished, the one called Finnen Lufkin would be only too gladly surrendered unto Her.

Spiraling around the oaks, listening to the shrill screams of the dying wer-rats, the messenger of the High Lady started to panic. The thorn ogres were out of control, and there was nothing it could do to halt the senseless, wasteful slaughter.

"Desist!" the owl squawked. "Thy mistress demands it! The one to whom the thief spoke with must be found. Ye will slay them all! Halt, I say! This is not what She planned!"

But the monarch of the Hollow Hill had furnished Her pets with meager minds, and they were inflamed with a craving for death and blood that no one could restrain.

"Hearken to me!" the owl screeched in vain. "Ye shall ruin all Her hopes and designs. Slay no more! Thy mistress needs to speak with them! Fools! Fools!"

Yet still the werlings continued to lose both the battle and their lives.

On the platform of the hazel, Stookie Maffin and her friends wept and wailed as dark, barbed shapes strode forward to crush them.

Stumpy legs pounded the decking, splintering the timbers as three repulsive apparitions lurched after the terrified youngsters, taunting and terrorizing them.

"Come to us," the ogres cackled in their hollow voices. "Come—sleep in our throats."

Screaming, Stookie stumbled and tripped, falling right into their path.

Greedy claws reached out to snatch her, when suddenly a frenzied blur of snowy feathers came diving between them.

"Hold!" the owl commanded. "I forbid thee to kill this creature. Thou must wait until thy mistress has learned all She desires. Then ye may all drown yourselves in barrels of wer-rat blood."

The ogre glared at the bird. It was too late now. They had tasted the sweet flavor of these tiny creatures, and the heinous spirits that Rhiannon had nourished within them would not be denied. With an impatient grunt the thorn monster batted the owl away and was incensed to discover that Stookie and her friends had escaped up into the overhanging branches.

Growling threateningly, the three ogres began tearing down the hazel twigs, ripping the tree apart until there would be no refuge left.

Elsewhere, in the wych elm, Krakkwhipp was basking in the fear flowing from the werlings it had hunted down. Its comrade was still chewing the remains of the defenders it had caught and sucking its fangs with disgusting relish.

Trapped against the elm's trunk, the Doolan family, Liffidia, and Tollychook all stared up into Krakkwhipp's dribbling jaws, unable to lift their eyes to the bodies still hanging from its spiky crown. Bufus's thoughts flew to his dead brother. Had Mufus been this afraid?

Across the woodland the desperate struggles for life were nearing their deadly conclusions. The thorn ogres were too formidable a foe for the small werlings to strive against.

In the Tumpin oak a gust of fetid breath blew upon the backs of Kernella's legs, and she turned to see Ungartakka's enormous pug face leering at her.

"Look out!" she cried to the others as a twitching claw came stretching for them.

Confronted by this new threat, they scattered in every direction. Some clambered up the trunk while others ran along the branches. The groping claw separated Kernella from the rest of her family, and driven back by the clutching talons, she was forced to disappear inside the entrance of the Tumpin home.

"No!" her mother called, remembering the fate of the Dritches. "Not in there!"

But Kernella was trapped and could not get out. The hooked claws of Ungartakka pushed into the passage, and Gamaliel and his parents could only watch in horror and wait for her screams.

Agonized wails ripped through the oak, but it was not Kernella's voice. It was the thorn ogre's.

Shrieking in torment, Ungartakka snatched its arm from the entrance. Its claw was smoking with flame.

"You come back here!" Kernella Tumpin cried, bustling out of the passage with a lantern in one hand and a fiery torch in the other.

The thorn ogre screeched, and the fires leaped the length of its arm. Over the gigantic head the flames went scorching, and in a moment the creature's entire bulk was burning.

Shrill and piercing were the screams that boiled from Ungartakka's sizzling jaws. Finally the talons holding the malignant creature to the oak withered in the heat, and it plunged to the ground.

Scampering over a branch to get a better view, Kernella watched the ogre hit the woodland floor. It exploded in a violent burst of flame that singed her eyebrows when the searing vapor came blasting upward.

"You knock next time!" she bawled.

Still floundering upon its back, Chokerstick was engulfed in the tumultuous fireball, and it, too, ignited. As a living bonfire it burned, but its anguished yowls lasted only until the furnace of its lungs collapsed. Then the crackling roar of the flames took over.

From that moment on, the werlings' fortunes turned.

When the others saw what Kernella had done, lamps and lanterns were immediately brandished in every treetop. The rampaging ogres were instantly dismayed, and they cringed and recoiled from the hungry flames.

Out of the branches they dropped, shriveling and burning. Bows were strung with flaming arrows that went sizzling into the tough bark of their hides, and set the devouring fires raging from within.

Soon the woodland thundered to the uproar of their

roasting. Demented with the terror of the flames, the thorn ogres bolted blindly, raving and shrieking.

From the wych elm of the Doolans, Krakkwhipp leaped, wreathed in a halo of fire. So ferociously did it rage that by the time it struck the ground, the creature was dead, and its charred carcass crumbled to ashes and cinders.

Columns of twisting black smoke wound about the trees as the yammering host took flight. To the stream they charged, and the werlings came rushing after them, shouting and waving their torches.

Hearing the strange new commotion, Yoori Mattock came racing from the underground council chamber, where he had found refuge. The ogre that had pursued him was already trampling toward the Hagburn. When he saw what was happening, Yoori punched the air and disappeared beneath the roots of the apple tree once more, only to emerge a minute later carrying a long staff bound about with rags that were blazing brightly. Then he ran after those monsters that had so far avoided the greedy flames, and with a vengeful cry, he set them on fire.

"Demon filth!" he cried when his erstwhile attacker burst into flame. Gabbling in fulminating agony, it ran to the banks of the stream, where it toppled from the edge but exploded before hitting the water.

"That's an end of it and the rest of them!" Mr. Mattock declared, throwing the flaming brand to the ground.

All of those werlings who were not injured or tending to the wounded gathered by the banks of the stream and gazed back at the smoking corpses of the enemy. Looking on those scattered piles of glowing cinders, every one of them was stunned and shocked. They did not know what those horrors had been or where they had come from. For the moment the fact that they had been defeated was enough.

From their oak the Tumpin family joined the crowding survivors.

Trailing behind them, Gamaliel looked down at his paws and felt the mouse's tail dragging over the ground. Now that the immediate danger was over, he knew he should return to his normal shape. But would he be able to?

Frighty Aggie had never managed to escape from her mongrel form. What if he was trapped like this forever?

Dawdling behind the others, he closed his eyes and murmured the simpler rhyme that Terser Gibble had taught to them.

"I call on ye who lay beneath, soil and sky, bark
    and leaf.
Unyoke flesh, unbar door,
Cast off shape and wear no more.
Give again the form that's good, by the might of
    great Hagwood."

Nothing happened. The tail still swished behind him, the feathers streamed and bobbed from the top of his snookulhood, and he felt the weight of the hedgehog prickles sticking from his back.

"I'm stuck," he breathed miserably. "Jammed in this 'orrible shape for the rest of my life. What am I going to do?"

Not wishing to reopen his eyes, he bowed his head.

The rest of his family had moved on ahead, but Kernella turned to see where her brother had got to, and a scowl clouded her singed face.

"Gamaliel Tumpin!" she bawled. "Stop idling and get here now!"

At the mention of his name, Gamaliel was immediately seized by quivering forces that sent sharp, needling pains from the tip of his tail up to the topmost feather on his head.

High into the air he leaped, juddering as each of the hedgehog spines went shooting back into his skin, and his long legs returned to normal. The sleek covering of fur shrank out of existence, and the feathers were replaced by his usual gingery hair. With a slap the mouse's tail disappeared, and when he landed back on the ground, he was back to his former self.

Dizzily, Gamaliel looked over to where Kernella was waiting with her arms folded, and he grinned at her.

"Good job she's so bossy after all!" he chuckled.


AND so the first battle ever to have been waged in that quiet corner of Hagwood had been won. Not one thorn ogre made it back across the Hagburn, and the fumes from their blackened remains sent a great reek pouring into the sky.

Diving through the choking smoke, its creamy feathers darkened by soot, the barn owl eyed the destruction of its mistress's forces with anger and contempt.

Circling over the realm of the werlings, it gazed upon the innumerable smoldering corpses and screeched bitterly.

The infernal army of the Lady Rhiannon was not the invincible horde She had believed them to be.

Beating its wings, the owl soared above the smoke and left that little land behind.

The wer-rats had proven more resilient than its mistress had anticipated. Those lowly creatures that had escaped Her notice these many years would have to be considered anew. The one called Finnen Lufkin must be found, and the casket containing the beating heart of the High Lady recovered.

That night in the Silent Grove, the bodies of those slain in the carnage were given to the beeches.

Forty-nine werlings had lost their lives that day. It was a grievous, evil time from which no one would ever truly recover.

As the sumptuous light of the last beech blossom dwindled and went out, Finnen Lufkin hung his head.

He had returned to find that the battle was over. When he had assured himself that his grandmother was safe, the boy had joined everyone else in the grim toil of picking through the burned carcasses of the thorn ogres to discover any other remains. The cleanup operations would commence tomorrow, but tonight the interments must take place.

Finnen's banishment had been lifted by Yoori Mattock, but his crime had not been forgiven. He was forbidden to enter the Silent Grove, and for that he was grateful.

Sitting beyond the brink of that hallowed dingle, in exactly the same spot where he had sat with the Wandering Smith only the night before, he watched as the mourning families began to depart.

Liffidia's fox cub lay at his side, waiting impatiently for its beloved mistress to return, and Finnen stroked it gently.

In the morning the council would meet, and this time they would listen to him. Their lives would never be the same again; the carefree existence they had enjoyed throughout the ages had gone forever. Henceforth, the werlings would have to arm themselves properly and learn how to fight. Wergling was no longer any protection.

The fox cub jolted and sat upright. Liffidia was leaving the grove with her mother, and the animal dashed across to greet her.

Finnen smiled faintly, then raised his hand and got to his feet, for a plump figure was striding purposefully toward him.

Wiping his eyes, Gamaliel Tumpin shook his head. "So many," he uttered, "and they were only the ones that could be found. They're saying that the real number of dead is more like sixty!"

"It's only the beginning," Finnen said darkly. "The High Lady won't stop now. She has other forces, other evils to send against us. We're at war, Gamaliel. She thinks we know where that casket is hidden. I wish the Smith had told us—I'd open that gold box and stick a knife in Her heart."

From his belt he took a silver-handled dagger that to him was more like a fat sword.

"Thimbleglaive!" Gamaliel cried in astonishment.

"I found it at the bottom of that hill," Finnen explained.

"Where it fell after the imp dropped it. Perhaps one day I'll be able to use it in a way that would make the Smith proud."

Gamaliel glanced nervously at his friend, then looked cautiously around them. When he was sure no one was watching, he whispered, "Maybe you will, because I've found something as well."

Finnen did not understand. Gamaliel's voice was grave and fearful and his eyes were glittering with excitement and dread. Opening the neck of his wergle pouch, Gamaliel reached inside.

"He must have put it here when he tended to my shoulder," he murmured. "That's the only time he could have. I discovered it this evening but haven't dared show or tell anyone yet. Oh, Finnen, what are we supposed to do?"

Slowly he withdrew his hand from the velvety bag and unfurled his fingers.

Finnen caught his breath, and his grip upon Thimbleglaive tightened as he saw.

It was a thing that the Wandering Smith had carried with him throughout the long years of his self-imposed exile: a precious, most valuable object. In the deep desperation of his last night upon this earth, with the enemy closing around him, the Pucca had entrusted it and all his hope to the small, insignificant race of werlings, so that they might continue should he fail.

For there, lying upon Gamaliel Tumpin's open palm, was a delicate and beautiful golden key.

*This is the first of The Hagwood Trilogy. The story will continue.*